FORTUNE

FALLS

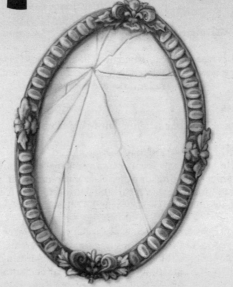

JENNY GOEBEL

SCHOLASTIC INC.

For my mom—
Thank you for teaching me the things worth believing in.

Copyright © 2016 by Jenny Goebel

This book was originally published in hardcover by Scholastic Press in 2016.

All rights reserved. Published by Scholastic Inc., *Publishers since 1920*. SCHOLASTIC and associated logos are trademarks and/or registered trademarks of Scholastic Inc.

The publisher does not have any control over and does not assume any responsibility for author or third-party websites or their content.

No part of this publication may be reproduced, stored in a retrieval system, or transmitted in any form or by any means, electronic, mechanical, photocopying, recording, or otherwise, without written permission of the publisher. For information regarding permission, write to Scholastic Inc., Attention: Permissions Department, 557 Broadway, New York, NY 10012.

This book is a work of fiction. Names, characters, places, and incidents are either the product of the author's imagination or are used fictitiously, and any resemblance to actual persons, living or dead, business establishments, events, or locales is entirely coincidental.

ISBN 978-1-338-13470-4

10 9 8 7 6 5 4 3 2 1   17 18 19 20 21

Printed in the U.S.A.   40
First printing 2017

Sometimes our fate resembles a fruit tree in winter. Who would think that those branches would turn green again and blossom, but we hope it, we know it.

—Johann Wolfgang von Goethe

1

STEP ON A CRACK

Petey's sweaty little hand wriggled in mine. It was hard to hold on to, like a fish fighting to make its way back into a pond. If we'd been anywhere else in town, I probably wouldn't have cared. I might even have let it go. Instead I said, "Petey, stop squirming." Then I reached over and clamped my free hand around his scrawny upper arm, preventing my five-year-old brother from writhing out of my grasp. When he looked up from under his mop of wayward curls, I tipped my head ever so slightly in the direction of Tommy's mom, Mrs. Mitchell. It was all the reminder Petey needed.

Mrs. Mitchell had just dropped Tommy off at the Pot-of-Gold Child Care Center and was walking away, but even from a distance, it was impossible to ignore the halo cast encasing her head and neck as her fractured vertebrae healed.

It might be called a halo cast, I thought, *but there is absolutely nothing holy about the medieval contraption screwed onto Mrs.*

Mitchell's skull. Unfortunately, it was all too common a sight in Fortune Falls.

"Come on, Petey," I said, collecting myself and turning my attention back to my brother.

But Petey's face was now ash gray, the same color as the cement we were attempting to traverse. His small blue sneakers were glued to a solid patch of it, and cracks sprawled like spiderwebs down the path in front of us. One false move, and somewhere across town, our own mother would feel something in her back snap, and crumple to the floor in agony.

"It's all right," I reassured him, even though the stretch of pavement between us and Petey's day care was particularly tricky. "Let's pretend it's just a game." I acted braver than I felt as I hopped to the next piece of solid ground, still gripping his hand tightly. Petey eyed me warily, unmoving.

"It's like hopscotch," I said. "Just don't land on a crack."

Petey glanced over his shoulder, in the direction we'd come from.

"Nope," I said with resolve. "If I have to go to school today, so do you. We're not going home." I hopped back next to him. "Shoelaces tied?" I lifted the bottoms of his pant legs to reveal the double knots I'd tied as securely as possible before we'd left the house. "Check. Path clear of leaves, twigs, and other tripping hazards?" We both scanned the sidewalk in front of us. "Check."

I cupped Petey's chin in my hand and waited until his hazel eyes were looking back into my own. "Trust me?" I asked.

The flicker of doubt I saw there was a stab to the heart. Even my young brother was starting to see me the way everyone else did—as a vacuum for bad luck, a magnet for misfortune. Maybe he'd never been worried that *his* misguided footstep would cause our mother to cry out in pain and fall to the cold tile floor at the hospital where she worked. Perhaps all along his fear had been that *I* would step on a crack and break our mother's back.

I wanted to remind him that I hadn't been tested yet. Technically, I was still classified as Undetermined, but we both knew that didn't matter. My hand felt detached from the rest of my body as it started to slip from Petey's. But then he squeezed it with a ferocity that surprised me, and squared his boney shoulders in stout determination. "Check," he said in his tiny boy voice. "I trust you, Sadie." And this time he took the first step.

As I approached the crosswalk in front of Fortune Falls Elementary a short while later, a commanding red hand popped up on the signal. I waited by the side of the road as a shiny, tanklike SUV with dark-tinted windows whizzed by.

I didn't have to see who was riding inside to know that Luckies had caused the light to change. The vehicle never slowed. Obviously they'd expected the light to turn green as they'd approached the intersection. Most lights probably did for them.

Sure enough, after the SUV whipped into the parking lot, I saw Ian Silverman vault flawlessly from the staggeringly tall vehicle and land with both feet squarely on the solid pavement.

Ian had been in my homeroom when we started school back in August, when we were all still Undetermined. However, he'd turned twelve in September, which meant he'd been part of the first wave to take the Luck Test.

No one was surprised when Ian passed with flying colors and was transferred to a homeroom for Luckies only. That's how it would go for the rest of the year. Every few months, a new group would take the test. Those who passed would go from Undetermineds to Luckies. Those who failed would be revealed as Unluckies. It might not seem like a big deal, having to switch homerooms, but that was only a temporary measure.

After sixth-grade graduation, the Luckies would move on to Flourish Academy, a day school. On the other hand, after the Unluckies graduated, they'd be shipped off to Bane's School for Luckless Adolescents—a boarding school designed to keep the Unluckies from endangering those around them. I'd never seen it with my own eyes, but I'd heard it was awful.

Ian ran over to the basketball court where Simon Swift was waiting. Simon was still Undetermined like me, but there was no reason for him to fear the Spring Luck Test, which was now only a week away. I watched as Ian and Simon began swishing ball after ball through the hoops. It didn't matter where they shot from—behind their back, a great distance away—it still went in. Simon even banked a shot off a nearby tree, something only a Lucky would be able to do. Something I couldn't do if my life depended on it.

It was mesmerizing to watch them play. The dribbling sounded so pleasantly rhythmic against the cacophony of chattering students waiting for the bell to ring. For just a moment, I allowed myself to be hypnotized by their fluid movements instead of thinking about what the next week might hold for me.

A wall of muddy water shook me back to reality. The splash was cold and sudden. I whipped around in shock only to have a second spray kicked up in my face.

If I hadn't been so entranced by Ian and Simon's game, I would've noticed the giant puddle in the gutter. Instead, I'd stood dumbly on the sidewalk nearby as one car, and then another, had driven through it. Now I was soaked and angry with myself for making such a careless mistake. Lights never magically turned green for me. I had to pay attention. I couldn't afford not to.

I wiped my eyes and lips with a dry spot on my sleeve, just as the bell rang and everyone else started piling in through the front doors. I sighed heavily. Mrs. Swinton wouldn't like it if I was late again, but she'd like it even less if I dripped dirty water all over the classroom carpet. So as the other students rushed off to their classrooms, I found my way to the girls' bathroom.

I spent the next ten minutes dabbing water off my clothes and wiping chunks of mud out of my hair. I splashed clean water onto my cheeks, but the mirror above the sink wasn't really a mirror at all, so I couldn't see if I'd gotten my face entirely clean.

An Unlucky student named Hannah accidentally broke the real mirror in the girls' bathroom two years ago. Not even an hour later, she was dead. A passing car had blown a tire, rammed through the fence, and crashed onto the playground. Hannah, sulking over the broken mirror, had been sitting close to the fence when the man's car broke through. The entire school was grief-stricken, but not entirely shocked. Breaking a mirror brought a seven-year curse—one of the worst in Fortune Falls—but most didn't outlive the duration. Still, Hannah's ruin had been particularly swift.

Two things changed after that. First, the Unluckies were no longer allowed on the playground at recess. Second, a construction worker removed the rest of the school mirrors and replaced them all with shiny metal sheeting. The metal sheeting was nearly indestructible, but it completely warped any reflections.

I could see a wobbly outline of my face, framed by my own unruly curls, but my features were all distorted and I couldn't tell if I'd missed any splatters of mud. It didn't matter, though, really. It's not like I could wash all the speckles off my cream-colored sweater or light blue jeans anyway. Or rinse all the Unlucky from my blood, for that matter. I'd have about as much luck doing that as a leopard would at changing its spots.

2

KNOCK ON WOOD

I left the girls' bathroom just in time to get caught in the small crowd of Unluckies slipping in through the side entrance of the school. I couldn't help but notice the way they stumbled along with their snotty noses, stained shirts, and Band-Aids galore. Was this a glimpse of my not-so-distant future?

One Unlucky student stepped on another's shoelace, and it started a chain reaction as a group of them tumbled like dominoes. That was why they used a separate entrance and had a later start time. So that they wouldn't hinder the other students. The idea was for the Unluckies to have as little contact with everyone else as possible until they were shipped off to Bane's School for Luckless Adolescents next fall.

The Luckies' parents made a huge fuss whenever they thought their fortuitous children were being jeopardized by an Unlucky. Sometimes, even parents of Undetermined kids complained. Rumor was that Felicia Kahn's mother and father had registered one hundred thirty-seven complaints so far this year. Most of their calls had been about me.

They claimed I was a danger to everyone around me. At least that's what they said at the beginning of the school year, right after I was blamed for the collapse of the gym bleachers.

They'd made a big to-do about the whole thing, even though faulty welding could've explained why it crumbled when I leaned on it. No one was too seriously injured, thankfully, and the goose egg on Felicia's forehead went away after about a week. So, really, they should've forgiven me for it by now.

Still, the Kahns had blabbered to anyone who would listen that I should be identified as Unlucky right away instead of waiting for the Spring Test. "Let's be honest," I'd overheard Felicia's mom saying to Principal Lyon, "Sadie was born on Friday the thirteenth, and her birthday lands on Friday, March thirteenth, again this year. Shouldn't that tell us *something*?"

I stopped in the middle of the hall and let the downtrodden pack sweep ahead of me. *One more week*, I reminded myself. I wasn't officially one of them yet. I had one more week to increase my luck, before I'd have to prove to everyone that I wasn't such a menace to society. Anything could happen in a week. Maybe, by some miracle, I *could* pass the test and go on to Flourish with my best friend, Cooper, and all the other Luckies.

Then I looked down and saw a patch of mud on my sleeve that I hadn't been able to wash out. Who was I trying to fool? I was destined for Bane's. With my shoulders slumped, I continued down the hall and turned the knob to open Mrs. Swinton's classroom door.

I held my breath and barged right in. If a lifetime of mishap and embarrassment had taught me anything, it was the quicker you got the discomfort over with, the better.

As expected, every single Undetermined student turned to look at me as Mrs. Swinton sighed loudly. In a voice that wasn't entirely unsympathetic, she said, "What was it this time, Sadie? Were you chased by a swarm of bees? Did you fall down an open manhole again?"

"Sorry, Mrs. Swinton. I—" But as soon as I opened my mouth, she cut me off.

"Look, Sadie, since you know *something* is going to happen to you on the way to school, can you at least try to leave earlier?" Mrs. Swinton's head hardly reached above the podium she stood behind. Nothing about her—from her close-cropped gray hair to her long, flowered skirt—seemed imposing. Yet the tight pinch to her lips and the edge, quite common in her voice, said she was a force to be reckoned with. "Please take your seat."

I nodded as I hurried past her, then scooted by four rows of desks. Fewer than half of the desks were occupied since most of our classmates had already been sorted into Luckies and Unluckies. Felicia whispered something to Betsy and Sabrina, and the three of them giggled. When I slid into my seat at the far back corner of the room, almost toppling my chair over backward in the process, Betsy stopped laughing. Felicia's and Sabrina's snickers grew into guffaws.

Mrs. Swinton cleared her throat. All three girls sat up, tall and studious-like, and I dropped my gaze to the empty desk next to mine, the one where my best friend used to sit.

I tried to picture his friendly face in place of the scornful glares Felicia shot when the teacher wasn't looking.

Cooper could do a terrific impression of a Lucky. If I was feeling low, he'd throw his arms up in mock indignation and say something like "Argh! I didn't win that contest I forgot to enter. I'm having such a bad day." Or "Can you believe the PTO president gave me chocolate cake for winning the cake walk? Doesn't he know lemon poppy seed is my favorite?" Then Cooper would draw his lips into a pout and wait until I cracked. It wouldn't matter how painful or embarrassing my day had been up until that point, in spite of myself, I'd laugh.

If only Cooper were still Undetermined.

No, I didn't mean that. I was glad he'd passed the Winter Test. I hadn't been sure that he would. Just, now that he was with the Luckies all day, I missed him terribly. And at least Felicia pretended to be nice when Cooper was around.

Mrs. Swinton stepped up to the whiteboard, and I snapped back to attention. It took me a minute to realize what she was doing. She was drawing a horseshoe in the upper right-hand corner of the board. "As you all are aware, the Spring Luck Test will take place next Monday, one week from today," she said. "I'll add a horseshoe every day. After we have seven of them, it will, of course, be the day of the test."

Seven was a lucky number. Seven lucky horseshoes. For the Fall Test, she'd drawn rainbows. Four-leaf clovers for the Winter one. It was a daily reminder to do everything we could to increase our luck between now and then.

"I've been blowing on my lucky dice every night before bed," a boy named Manuel whispered to another boy, Nathan Small. Nathan's eyes flicked in Manuel's direction, but he seemed too filled with worry to speak.

"You can't even use your own dice on the test, stupid," Sabrina interjected.

"I know, but—"

"That's enough," Mrs. Swinton said reproachfully. "I just hope that all of you remembered to use your birthday wishes wisely and didn't squander them away on frivolous things."

At this, Nathan buried his face in his hands, and I recalled him bragging about a new gaming system after he turned twelve last month. Quite a few others students were fidgeting in their seats, and there were more fingers crossed than I could quickly count. Most of the squirmers were ones I would've expected to be nervous, like me. However, the beads of sweat on Betsy Williams's freckled forehead surprised me.

I double-checked the birthday calendar pinned to the wall. Nope. My name was the only one written in smudged black dry-erase marker for this week. That meant, considering all the anxiety hanging in the air, a good number of students had wasted their wishes when they'd turned twelve— or perhaps they hadn't been able to make their wishes at all. I knew far too well how difficult it could be to blow out all your candles, no matter how seriously you took the task.

My stomach muscles constricted, and my heart pounded in my chest. Not this year. This year, I had to earn my wish, even if my birthday did land on Friday the thirteenth. Then I had to use my wish to pass the Luck Test. I just had to. If I didn't . . . if I failed the test and was sent to Bane's . . . I didn't even want to think about what that would be like.

My blood pulsed even harder as Mrs. Swinton launched into a speech we'd heard two times already—when she was prepping the students who'd taken the Fall and Winter Tests. I think it was supposed to be inspiring, but really, it only fueled my sensation of falling off a cliff. Especially when she said things like "Pass the test and you will prosper. Fail and you'll find nothing but a lifetime of desolation."

Then I made the mistake of glancing at Felicia and Sabrina. The two of them were leaning back in their chairs, smirking and purposely stretching out their graceful swan arms, as if to show that they were above such ridiculousness as finger crossing. Those two had so much good kismet it was coming out of their ears—in Felicia's case, literally. Dangly jade earrings hung like teardrops near the delicate slopes of Felicia's jawbones, accented even more by her high, sleek black ponytail.

In Fortune Falls, jade cost more than diamonds. But so did a lot of things: four-leaf clovers, horseshoes, and rabbits' feet, just to name a few. All Felicia would have to do is show up for the Luck Test in those lucky earrings, and she'd breeze right through. She'd probably even used her birthday wish on the matching new green cashmere sweater she was wearing and thought nothing of it.

Mrs. Swinton's lips pursed at the corners as she said, "But I'm sure none of you have anything to worry about. You'll all do just fine on your upcoming tests."

The air tingled with energy as every single student formed a tight fist and rapped their knuckles on wood, three times in perfect unison.

No one dared to flat-out ignore the bold statement, but some took it more lightly than others. Simon Swift yawned into his basketball shooting hand while knocking with the other. Felicia and Sabrina rolled their eyes. The less confident among us—anyone who had poor luck to begin with, as well as those on the fringe who might've botched their birthday wishes—performed the ritual with such intense reverence, it seemed almost like prayer.

Mrs. Swinton gave a quick, approving nod of her head, and then got down to business. "Now, who can tell me what 567,690 divided by 894 is?"

Like most everyone else, I immediately began rummaging through my desk for a pencil and a sheet of paper, but Felicia's hand shot straight up into the air.

"Felicia?" Mrs. Swinton said.

"Hmmm . . . 635?" Felicia gave her answer in such a way that it was clear she was just plucking a number out of her head. Then excitedly she added, "Am I right?"

"Yes, Felicia. Lucky guess," Mrs. Swinton said flatly. The rest of us dropped our pencils. "Okay, why don't we try taking out our math books instead? Please find page 203 and complete problems one through thirty."

I know it's weird, but getting started on the assignment was a relief. It loosened my stomach muscles and slowed my heartbeat. For the first time all morning, I felt somewhat at ease. I couldn't make random guesses and get the answers right the way Felicia could, but schoolwork typically came easy to me. It wasn't all murky like Fate, and luck, and superstitions. It had right and wrong answers. And grades, for the most part, weren't determined by what charms you owned, or whether or not you toppled over the saltshaker at breakfast.

Throwing myself completely into the problems at hand (those of the long-division variety), I was almost able to forget about my birthday on Friday, and the test next Monday, and the fact that Cooper's parents were being swayed by the Kahns and already didn't want him hanging out with me.

I could almost forget about all the bad things that had happened to me and the people I loved, and that a year from now I'd probably be living at Bane's—only able to see Petey and my mom every now and then. As for my dog and Cooper— I'd probably never get to see either of them.

I could almost forget about all the ways my terrible luck was threatening to sink me. *Almost*.

Right before we were supposed to head to the cafeteria, Mrs. Swinton said, "Felicia Kahn and Sadie Bleeker, I'd like to see both of you after everyone else leaves for lunch."

I was more surprised than worried. Felicia and I were hardly ever clumped together. In a daze, I wandered toward Mrs. Swinton's desk as the room emptied out.

From the way Felicia was examining the muddy spots on my clothing and then turning her nose up in the air, I'd have to say *appalled* was a better word than *surprised* for what she was feeling.

"Ladies," Mrs. Swinton said after the door shut. "I've graded the quizzes you took last week. Congratulations, you've both qualified for the school spelling bee."

"What?" Felicia said sharply. "How did *she* qualify?"

Honestly, I wasn't even offended. I was sort of wondering the same thing.

Mrs. Swinton raised an eyebrow. "Don't confuse an aptitude for spelling with luck, Felicia."

"When is it?" I asked. I felt stunned, sickened even.

"This Thursday," Mrs. Swinton said. "There will be two representatives from every homeroom. It will take place in the gym, in front of the entire school, and the winner will move on to the district bee taking place next month."

"Unluckies, too?" Felicia's asked, the look on her face growing more revolted.

Mrs. Swinton sighed. "No, of course not, Felicia. Only Luckies and students who are Undetermined."

"But—"

The teacher held up her hand. "Sadie is still Undetermined, just like you. However, I'm afraid that any contestant who fails the Luck Test will be automatically disqualified and will not be allowed to participate next month at districts."

It was harsh, but I understood. It'd be too dangerous for a real Unlucky—not just an Undetermined like me—to be around that many other kids, no matter how great they were at spelling.

"So, really, what you're saying is that our classroom only has one true competitor." Felicia's grimace relaxed, and her mouth spread into an arrogant smile. She knew I had no chance of passing the test.

"That's not what I'm saying at all," Mrs. Swinton replied with a finality that left no room for argument. "Now the two of you should go to lunch."

I hung back as Felicia promenaded out of the classroom. She made my blood boil. I knew I was a better speller than she was, but I'd stopped wanting to be on any sort of stage a long time ago. Plus, the last thing I needed right now was a distraction. My mud-splattered clothes were a perfect reminder of that. No, the only thing I had time to concentrate on this week was finding a way to pass the Luck Test.

3

LUCKY PENNY

Petey had a good day, a purple day, his preschool teacher said. At first, I thought Ms. Summer was referring to the purple paint splatters in Petey's curly light brown hair—hair the exact same color and texture as my own.

Ms. Summer's hair, on the other hand, was a rich chestnut, and it fell into a perfect bob just below her chin. With hair like that, not a single strand out of place, she had to be a Lucky. *Which is a good thing*, I reminded myself. *Petey's stuck with me all the time. The last thing he needs is a hapless person looking after him at school, too.*

It was only when Ms. Summer pointed to a clipboard with a rainbow-colored behavior chart that I realized what she meant. "Purple is the highest level," she said, beaming appreciatively at my little brother. I was slightly taken aback. It was not a look people often gave us Bleekers.

"Um . . . what about the paint?" I asked, thinking she

must've gotten Petey mixed up with one of the other preschoolers.

"Another child's art project gone terribly wrong, I'm afraid," Ms. Summer said, and then clicked her tongue. Now, that was a sound I was used to.

Petey and I made it back across the splintered cement we'd crossed that morning—again without stepping on a single crack. When the sidewalk curved to the right, we continued going straight. The dirt path that ran behind a row of houses with large yards and pretty shutters on the windows was a far safer route for the two of us.

Since I didn't have to worry about breaking my mother's back just then, I allowed myself to ponder what it might mean to have a Lucky for a brother. I'd always assumed Petey would veer toward hapless like the rest of the family. Not that Mom or Dad had ever been tested. The Luck Test was enacted after my parents were out of school and married, which meant most of the adults in town hadn't been tested, either. It only wormed its way into the school system nine years ago after a boy named John Floyd turned thirteen and nearly reduced his entire neighborhood to ashes. All it took was a gas leak and a few birthday candles, and a ball of flames engulfed his home. It was a windy day. The fire spread quickly. The school board president's house could not be saved.

Still, test or no test, my parents were clearly ill-starred. They'd had me for a daughter, hadn't they? But what if Petey wasn't? What if he could sail through life without worrying that doom lay around each and every corner? What would that even feel like?

The truth was, I could remember the last time someone had looked at me the way Ms. Summer had looked at Petey—as though somewhere inside there might be a streak of good fortune. It was the last time I'd truly felt lucky. I could also remember how quickly that feeling had changed.

Dad and I had been taking Wink for a walk when a tawny bird jolted up from the pebbly, dry riverbed in front of us. It flapped its wings, but instead of taking flight, it began staggering around unsteadily on absurdly long legs.

I'd let out a cry, thinking the bird must've been injured.

Dad had only laughed. "It's a killdeer, Sadie girl. She's just pretending to be hurt to lead us away from her nest. Probably thinks Wink, the one-eyed wonder dog, is searching for her next meal. Really laying it on thick, aren't you, mama bird?"

As the killdeer continued with her award-winning performance, I spotted exactly what she didn't want us to see. "Look!" I said, forging ahead. "The killdeer's eggs—I didn't know birds ever built their nests on the ground."

Dad nodded. "Some do," he said, and smiled at me

proudly. "Maybe you're a Lucky, happening upon one so easily."

The possibility of it had made me feel as though I had a hot-air balloon inside, ready to lift me off the ground. I'd felt so deliciously light and happy then.

Glancing down again at the purple clumps in Petey's hair, I wished like mad I could cinch the memory off there. But this memory was like a landslide, and I just couldn't stop the rest of it from barreling me over.

"I'd better not get too close with Wink here," Dad had continued. "Plus, their mama does seem to be rather distressed. We should probably move on . . ."

As I'd turned to do just that, I accidentally kicked up a small round pebble with one sneaker and it rolled beneath the other. Next thing I knew, I was stumbling and then lurching forward, trying to regain my balance—which I did, finally—when one foot landed squarely in the center of the killdeer's nest.

I felt the crunching beneath my misplaced sneaker before anything else. Before my dad and Wink were trotting up beside me, before the mama bird gave one last despondent squawk and before the crack of lives ending along with their fragile eggshells reached my ears.

My seven-year-old self slammed my eyes shut and stubbornly refused to open them as hot tears slid down my face.

Countless stained dresses, falls from bed, a twisted ankle the day before a ballet recital—this was just the latest on a long list of accidents my family had been trying to explain away for ages.

"Shhh," my dad had soothed, and tried to smooth my unmanageable curls with his hand. Wink licked at my knee. "Listen to me, Sadie girl," Dad said. "Even if you aren't lucky, you're smart, and that's far more important."

I soaked in his words, trying to let them patch the punctured balloon inside me. It never truly worked, though; something always happened that seemed to rip the seams wide open again. But for a long time—maybe even up until the day Dad died—I was foolish enough to believe I might someday be mended.

Petey gave my hand a tense squeeze, drawing me back to the present day. "Sadie, we're almost there."

Of course we were. Part of my superbly awful lot in life included living on the far side of Fortune Falls Cemetery. It was bad enough that my brother and I were forced to navigate the most treacherous stretch of sidewalk on a near-daily basis, but we also had to trek past the gates of the old graveyard each day on the way home from school.

Fading ribbons were tied to the cemetery fence posts and wilted flowers were scattered beside the path, but I knew that none of these memorials had been left for those buried inside.

Pass the graveyard, hold your breath,
Lest you wish to dance with Death.

The rhyme was taught to all children in Fortune Falls, and yet people still perished along this route. Before they closed the street, cars would break down and the drivers would panic, forgetting to hold their breath while they ran toward safety. The road was now its own graveyard of abandoned vehicles. Even the fire and police departments wouldn't respond to an emergency anywhere in the vicinity.

The footpath was much more direct and therefore much shorter. If you were a fast walker, you'd only have to hold your breath for about twenty seconds. But if the makeshift memorials were any indication, mishaps still occurred. At least this path was more accessible than the road, and the bodies had been cleared. I didn't think I could trust myself to walk down a path littered with bones every day and not scream.

"Are you ready?" I asked Petey.

He shook his head.

"Okay, then we'll wait until you are."

Petey's slight little frame heaved with relief. He flashed me a puny, crooked smile and then bounded off for a nearby tree.

Oh boy, I thought to myself, *this tree is going to be the downfall of Petey's good day.* I pictured him with his arm in a sling, and chased after my brother. When I reached the magnificent old oak, he'd already scrambled up three branches, and there was no way I was fortified with enough luck for tree climbing.

"Petey!" I yelled.

"You can see inside the cemetery from up here," he hollered back.

"I don't want to see inside the cemetery. I want you to come down!"

"It's like a lost city! There are vines on all the crosses. And like half of the headstones are broken or falling down."

"There's a reason everyone gets cremated these days," I nearly screamed. "And if you're not careful, you're going to be one of them very soon!"

Petey made no attempt to come down. Instead he said, "Hey, some big kids are coming this way."

In Petey's world, *big kid* could mean anyone a year older than he was to someone three times his age. Instinctively, I ducked behind the oak. "What do they look like?"

"Three girls."

That ruled out the only "big kid" in town I cared to see. "Stay quiet," I whisper-yelled. Then, without really thinking about what I was saying, I added, "With any luck they'll pass us by."

"But—"

"Hush!"

With Petey silenced, I could make out three high-pitched voices growing louder as the girls drew closer. I peeked out from my hiding spot just as Felicia Kahn stopped walking. She stooped over to pick something off the ground and then straightened up with a small, shiny coin in her hand. All three girls let out earsplitting squeals.

"I can't believe it," Sabrina said. "That is your second one today. You are SO lucky." The smile on her face couldn't hide her envy. Sabrina may have had fairy-tale golden locks and a cute little elfin nose, but even among those with luck, fortune seemed allotted by degrees, and everybody wanted more.

Betsy Williams was with them, too, but unlike Sabrina, she had no chance of usurping Felicia's role as Fortune Falls's most favored darling. "You're the luckiest," Betsy said wistfully, mirroring my thoughts exactly.

I really could've used that lucky penny.

Felicia didn't deny what Betsy had said. Instead she appeared to be attempting a demure smile, but like most everything about Felicia, it came off looking smug. She sighed loudly. "I can't believe Cooper hasn't asked me to the Friday the Thirteenth Dance already. But since he hasn't, this would be a very good day to bump into him. I mean, two lucky pennies in one day—there's no way he can resist me."

Felicia flicked her silky black ponytail over her left shoulder. Her flawless ivory complexion nearly gleamed in the late-afternoon sun. My heart sank. I wouldn't blame Cooper if he asked her. He deserved to go to the dance with the luckiest girl in town, and it's not like I could even attend if he asked me.

There was the matter of his parents actually *forbidding* him from hanging out with me. Even though the dance fell on my birthday this year, they would never allow him to spend it in my company. And then, of course, the Friday the Thirteenth Dance was really just a slap in the face to the unluckiest. It was too dangerous for any of us to even dream of going outside that day.

I noticed then that Betsy was frozen in place, petrified as she examined all the memorials adorning the path.

Felicia seemed to notice, too. "You go first, Betsy. That way if you have trouble, we can go for help," she said. I wondered if what she really meant was, *if you have trouble, we won't get stuck in the middle of it.* Any help Felicia and Sabrina could "go for" would arrive too late.

I felt sorry for Betsy as she timidly stepped forward. Like Cooper, Betsy had always been on the fringe—in that gray area—certainly not unlucky, but with no kismet to spare, either.

I wondered why Felicia even kept Betsy around. Maybe it was because next to Betsy she could shine even more brightly without any real risk of misfortune spilling over onto Felicia's shoes, ruining her dressy patent-leather flats.

Betsy must not have been moving quickly enough for Felicia, because she reached out and gave her friend a little nudge. Terror flooded Betsy's dull brown eyes. But she sucked in a large breath of air, then bravely darted across the path running directly in front of the falling-down twisted-iron gates. I couldn't help but hold my breath right along with her.

"You know she's never going to pass the Spring Luck Test, don't you?" Sabrina said to Felicia once Betsy was out of earshot.

Felicia chuckled snidely. "Of course I do. But if everyone passed, that would sort of defeat the purpose. Do you know what she wasted her birthday wish on?"

Sabrina shook her head.

"I'll tell you later. Right now, I need to find a certain boy before the luck from this penny wears off!" Felicia sucked in her breath and bolted past the gates. Sabrina did the same.

When I was certain they were gone, I let out a long sigh. "Climb down, Petey. Please," I said, reaching up to take hold of the first branch. It snapped off in my hand, and I fell backward, my head landing with a loud *thunk* on a rock beneath the tree. The branch fell on top of me, knocking the wind out of my lungs.

Petey clambered down with ease and was beside me before the world came back into focus. "Sadie, are you okay?"

I would have nodded my head, but it was throbbing. I shoved the branch off my stomach so I could breathe again. "I will be," I said, and then murmured to myself, "this time."

Petey helped me to my feet. Although, really, it was more just me holding on to his hand as I struggled to find solid footing. Waiting for the scenery to stop spinning, I noticed that my little brother was trembling beside me. His eyes were darting back and forth between me and the entrance to the cemetery we still had to pass.

"I'll be all right. Just give me minute." After a short pause, when the earth had finally stopped roiling beneath me, I added, "On the count of three?"

Petey nodded. We counted together, then sucked in as much air as either of us could hold. As we raced past the old iron gate, I glanced down at my little brother with his cheeks all puffed out with air.

Maybe failing the Luck Test wasn't the worst thing that could happen. Maybe it would even be for the better if I was sent off to Bane's—for Petey's sake, at least. Nothing terrified me more than the thought that my bad luck might cause him to meet the same fate as our father.

4

AN APPLE A DAY

Arriving home with nothing more than a bump on the back of my head was a huge relief. Arriving home to find Cooper on my front lawn was as good as stumbling upon a four-leaf clover. Just one look at his face—his rich brown skin and long dark eyelashes—made me feel happier inside. And, as any hapless person knows, happy is a close brethren to lucky.

Cooper had let Wink out of the backyard, and she was rolling around on the grass—her back right paw punching the air, rapid-fire, as he scratched behind her ear.

Wink makes most people uncomfortable. She makes them especially uncomfortable when her missing eye takes them by surprise. I'll be taking Wink for a walk and someone will come up to her at just the right angle (the angle from which she looks perfectly normal), but when she turns to greet the person—her tail wagging so hard it shakes her entire backside—giving whoever it is a full view of her one-eyed, pirate-y face, the stranger usually flips.

Some people try to hide their shock. And you'd think that expressions frozen in place would be better than sneers of revulsion, but they're not. The people who turn to ice are usually the same people who milliseconds before had been reaching out to pet Wink. When they freeze, their hands naturally fall back to their sides. In my opinion, those reactions are the worst, because they came so close. If the people had only stretched their hands a little farther, run their fingers through her short, soft fur, then they'd have realized that she's no monster. She's just like every other dog. Minus an eye.

Cooper has always seemed to get that. He's never pulled his hand back. Never has looked repulsed, either. The first time he met Wink, he reached right past her bum eye and found the sweet spot behind her ear. The spot that sent her leg thrumming in doggish glee to a beat the rest of us couldn't hear.

As Petey and I approached the lawn, Wink turned her head to face us, and her tongue lolled from the left side of her mouth. With her one good eye, she gave me a look that said, "I love this guy. You know I love this guy. Why have you been keeping him from me?" Like I was the one who'd told Cooper he couldn't visit.

"Cooper!" Petey cried, breaking free from my grasp. He bowled over Wink and tackled my best friend with a bear hug, just like he'd done countless times before. In that moment, I wanted nothing more than to pretend that things were like they'd always been. That I could invite Cooper to stay for a while, maybe even go inside and work on homework together like we used to.

As Cooper and Petey wrestled around on the grass, with Wink doing her best to join in on the fun, I felt my spirits lifting. That was the thing about Cooper. Even when Wink pinned his bright orange shirt with her paw while Petey dragged him in the opposite direction, ripping a hole along the bottom seam, Cooper beamed like he was having the grandest time of his life.

For a second, I was tempted to join in. I could tousle Petey's curls right along with Cooper as we all dodged a lashing from Wink's wagging tail. Then I remembered the last time my friend stuck around for an afternoon. He wound up needing eleven stiches.

Of course it was my fault. *It was always my fault.*

A few months back, I'd tried to take a seat next to him at our kitchen table—something a Lucky could do a million times and never have a problem. But when I sat down, one of the wooden chair legs splintered in half. I tumbled backward, slamming hard into the wall. The force of the impact left an ugly purple bruise on my left shoulder, but, worse, it knocked a picture frame off a nail. A sharp pointy corner of the frame came down right on top of Cooper's head and, well, you know the rest.

No. His parents were right. It was too dangerous for us to be friends.

I cleared my throat loudly, and the commotion on the front lawn came to a dwindling halt. "Petey and I need to go inside now," I said stiffly. But when I saw how Cooper's dark brown eyes sunk inward with disappointment, I added, "I'm glad you came . . . Wink's really happy to see you." On cue, my dog slathered saliva across Cooper's face with her tongue.

He gently nudged her away as he wiped his face with a now-holey T-shirt, and then pulled himself to his feet.

Before I could stop myself, the words "I'm happy to see you, too" slipped out of my mouth, and blood rushed to my cheeks.

He took a step toward me as Petey and Wink went back to tumbling around on the front lawn. "That's why I'm here."

"Oh?" I said, and bit my lip. As much as I wanted him to stay, I knew it was better not to encourage him. Petey was stuck with me, but that didn't mean Cooper should have to put up with any more of my calamity-causing ways.

"I looked for you at lunch, but—"

"I have a lot of homework," I blurted out. "I really should get started."

A flicker of doubt seemed to tug at the corners of his mouth. Perhaps he was wondering why I was trying to brush him off or maybe he was remembering a warning his parents had given him. Whatever it was, it didn't last long. His lips stretched into a grin as he said, "Okay, sure . . . I'll get going, *but* only if you promise to meet me at the tree house tonight. Eight o'clock sharp."

I sucked in air. So much air that I didn't have enough room in my lungs when I said, "But your parents—"

"Are going out to dinner," he said, still grinning.

"But aren't you worried—"

"That we'll have entirely too much fun? It is a valid concern."

I shook my head. "I can't."

"You can and you must." I caught a twinkle in his eyes. "That is, if you want a real shot at ending this nasty bad-luck streak you're having." Cooper always referred to my doomed situation as "a streak," like it was something that could be broken, and not a lifelong condition.

I might've felt more inclined to believe him if he wasn't constantly plotting ways to improve my fortune, always to no avail. We'd spent an entire afternoon once, walking until we both had blisters, with him no more than two feet in front of me, dropping pennies the entire time. *Tails.* Time after time, every last darn penny fell on unlucky tails.

There was no end to it, no escaping my terrible fate. But just as I was about to tell him as much, a flash of lightning followed by a deep rumbling clap of thunder electrified the air. The hairs on my arms stood on end—the strike was that close. My hands jerked up, as if I could brace myself for the troubling change in weather. Petey darted back to my side, and Wink cowered low to the ground, whimpering. She looked apologetic now, like she'd somehow angered the sky and this was her punishment.

Wink. I could see in her eye that she was getting ready to bolt. And racing after her in a lighting storm wasn't something that would go well for either of us. I lunged for her, but she tore away from my grasp. Poor girl was so spooked, she didn't know I was only trying to help. Cooper made a dive for her after I missed. Hooking his fingers through her collar, he caught Wink midstride and pulled her back beside us.

"Thanks," I said as he transferred his hold on Wink to me. "About tonight . . ." I began, but then the rain started. Droplets the size of pennies fell from the sky, pelting our skin, hair, and clothing, and leaving wet matted streaks down Wink's back. Her whimpers grew louder.

"Sadie?" Petey's voice quavered as he screeched out my name. He liked being wet about as much as Wink liked lightning.

"The tree house. Tonight, Sadie, be there," Cooper said. "Please." Then, with one last reassuring scratch behind Wink's ear, and an actual wink directed at Petey who stood half hidden behind my back, Cooper took off. The pace with which he ran through the rain stole my breath away. Yet every one of his strides fell perfectly between the cracks in the sidewalk. I know because I watched until he turned the corner and was gone from sight.

"Sadie," Petey said again, his voice no more stable than before. I nodded, and then we all darted across the wet grass and right through the front door.

Wink wasted no time shaking the water from her fur. The spray might've been annoying if Petey and I weren't both already sopping wet. Then she made a beeline down the hall and headed straight for the bathroom. I could hear her claws clicking on the porcelain, like silverware clinking together, as she settled into her usual hiding place. The bathtub was her sanctuary. It's where she'd wait out the storm.

I glanced down at Petey. The rain had rinsed the purple paint from his curls and plastered them flat against his head. I touched my fingers to my own hair. The moisture had puffed my curls out like Frankenstein's bride. I sighed. "Let's go get a snack."

"Dry off first?" Petey begged.

"In the kitchen."

My little brother scuttled behind me as we both left drip marks on the creaky, old floorboards leading down the hall. Just inside the cramped kitchen, I snagged a towel from a hook by the sink. The dish towel was white with a giant four-leaf clover that had been stitched on with green thread. Unfortunately, only the real thing counted.

I patted Petey dry first and hadn't even started drying myself when he began whining for cheesy puffs.

"Uh-uh, you know the routine. An apple a day . . ."

"Keeps the doctor away," he deadpanned.

"Eat your apple first. Then cheesy puffs." Returning the towel to its hook, I plucked a Red Delicious from the fruit basket on the counter and tossed it to him before grabbing one for myself. As we listened to the patter of the raindrops and watched the flashes of lightning illuminate the world beyond the windowpanes, we polished off our apples in silence.

Every once in a while a *boom* would rattle the windows, and a soft whine would echo in the bathtub. The whimpering noises bothered us more.

When there was nothing but cores left, Petey dug into the bag of cheesy puffs, and I dug into my homework. *Nothing like writing a social studies essay to distract me from my problems*, I thought. I should've known better. My report was on the thirteen original colonies, and my pen spurted blue ink everywhere just as I was writing the number thirteen for the thirteenth time.

That's how you know your luck is truly corroded, and it's not just that you're clumsy. Everybody makes mistakes. Everyone has accidents. And sometimes terrible things happen that are beyond anyone's control. But bad luck is different. Bad luck feels like Fate keeping tabs on you, playing cruel jokes and pulling strings, laughing at your expense while it does everything within its far-reaching power to make your life miserable.

I jumped up from the kitchen table and grabbed a paper towel to blot the blue puddle off my paper as quickly as possible. It was no use. The paper was ruined.

After I cleaned up the mess, I grabbed a fresh sheet of lined paper and a new ballpoint pen and started completely over. This time, I revised the report so that it only contained twelve mentions of the unlucky number. As I neatly rewrote the paper, the storm outside ended just as quickly as it had started.

The rain quit pouring, the sky stopped flashing, and Wink wandered out of the bathroom. Happy as a Lucky, she licked cheesy powder off Petey's fingers until I told him to go wash his hands. As soon as my little brother got up to go to the sink, Wink came over and rested her head on my thigh. She stayed that way until I finished my homework—long after

Petey had finished his snack and had headed to his room to play.

When she wasn't hiding in the bathtub, this was something Wink did—lay her head on my leg. Most of the time, I think I took her being there for granted. Today, it caused a lump to form in my throat. The test was coming so soon. Just one week away. And I knew how lost I'd feel without her if I was sent to live at Bane's. I thought she might feel a little lost without me, too.

After carefully tucking my homework inside my folder, I turned my full attention to Wink. Any scorn for the lapse in Cooper's visits had vanished from her eye. I petted her head and down the back of her neck. She shivered with pleasure.

Honestly, the worst kind of reaction a person can have to her disability isn't dropping a hand away, not petting her. The worst reaction a person can have is disappointment. And that was exactly what I'd felt when Dad brought her home almost five years ago today.

I still felt guilty for it.

Wink was supposed to be a surprise, but I knew something was up when a lady from the shelter called. I didn't answer the phone when it rang, but she left a voice mail reminding Dad to give "his new puppy her medicine."

A puppy! My heart had trilled with excitement. My birthday was only a few days away. I'd always wanted a puppy, and my new baby brother just wasn't cutting it. I bounced on my toes waiting by the door, trying to picture the puppy before she arrived. Would she have light-colored hair, frothy and curly like mine, or sleek brown fur? Would she be small or large? Have a long nose or a short, stubby muzzle? I decided it didn't matter what the puppy looked like; I loved her already.

At least I thought I did. When Dad walked through the door, I took one look at the puppy in his arms, at the caved-in side of her head where her other eye should've been, and at the puffy pink scar where her skin had been stitched back together and where fur would never grow, and I burst into tears.

I already had plenty of one-eyed dolls and Barbies with missing limbs. I didn't need anything else in my life that was flawed.

"Take her back!" I cried.

"Sadie girl!" Dad said admonishingly.

I scowled and ran from the room.

It took days of Wink wagging a hopeful tail as she nudged me with her nose for me to decide she wasn't actually defective. Her nose, by the way, is decidedly medium in size, as is she. And her fur isn't white or curly or brown—it's the color of fading sunlight and as soft as dandelion parachutes. She's perfect. When I finally did cave, I fell for her hard.

Dad told me later that no one else had wanted Wink and that he couldn't bear to leave her behind at the shelter. And with the surgery to remove her infected eye, and the medication we gave her afterward, she was fine.

"You're more than fine, aren't you, girl?" I said and cupped her face in my hand. "You're just like Dad said, you're a wonder."

Wink panted in agreement and I folded my body over hers, resting my cheek on top of her head. I couldn't imagine my life without her, or how much I'd miss her if I was forced to live at Bane's.

My thoughts drifted to what else I'd be forced to give up if I failed the test on Monday. My home. My family. My best friend. I also thought about what Cooper had said earlier. Was it possible that he could have found the right charm to rid me of my bad luck?

Something stirred in my chest as though a tiny puff of air had blown through that punctured balloon. I nestled even closer to my dog and whispered, "Please, oh please, let it be true."

5

SEVEN YEARS BAD LUCK

Wink scampered behind me as I left the kitchen to check on Petey. I found my brother sprawled across his bedroom floor, surrounded by a fortress of blocks. He didn't even look up as I poked my head in the door, while Wink ran over and curled up protectively beside him. Satisfied, I retreated to the basement.

Petey's room used to be my room, too. It had been my parents' idea for me to move out. When I turned ten, they said I was too old to share a bedroom with my little brother. I'm sure what they really meant was I was too unlucky. Either way, I wasn't happy about it. At first.

Because my new room is below ground level, the only window peers out at a not-so-lovely view of corrugated aluminum. And just outside the room, it's all rafters full of cobwebs and hard concrete floors. In a way, I felt like I was being banished.

It didn't take long, though, for me to settle in and to realize that I was really, truly happier in the basement.

When I was younger, I could never seem to remember to get out of bed on the same side I'd gotten in. (Yet another important rule for anyone Fate has lined up in its crosshairs.) So after a few twisted ankles and even a broken collarbone, I started sleeping on the floor.

When I moved to the basement, there was enough room to push a bed snug against the wall. That way there was really just one option for hopping out. I'd never had a dresser before, either. Again, because of space, but also because they were easy to pull over and had really sharp edges.

Dad said I couldn't live my life avoiding every risk—we just had to make a few adjustments. So we draped a padded quilt over the corners of my new armoire and filled the rest of the room with soft blue blankets and pillows the color of amethyst. We also painted the walls a pale purple, my favorite color, and dotted them with yellow bursts to look like stars. Now I didn't think about me being separated anymore or about everything being cushioned because I was unlucky. I just felt safe. Wink had her bathtub; I had my bedroom.

From what I'd heard about Bane's, they'd taken the opposite approach. The rooms there were anything but cozy. Students were only allowed to bring a few preapproved personal items, and the boarding rooms were almost entirely barren—every last potential hazard removed. It probably felt safe, too, but I couldn't imagine a place like that ever feeling like home.

My clothes were still spotted with mud from the puddle, so I changed and decided to start a load of laundry. I stepped out of my room, over a joint in the concrete floor, and up to our washer and dryer. As I dumped a bushel full into the washer, a sock slipped down through the opening between the two appliances. It was a tight fit, but I was able to wriggle my hand inside the gap. When I grabbed the sock, I caught a glimpse of another behind it. It was a bit of a stretch, but at last, I snatched the second sock with my fingertips and fished it out as well.

I took one glance at the second sock and lowered myself to a seated position on the hard slab of cement in front of the dryer.

Dad's sock.

I rubbed the striped wool between my forefinger and my thumb and smiled wistfully. It was soft and warm, nothing at all like the concrete beneath me.

Dad wouldn't have known it was missing, never would've tried to go looking for it, even if he'd had the chance. In all my life, I'd never known him to wear a pair of socks that matched.

He claimed mismatched socks were good luck—who knew if he was right or not. Beyond the basics, people held all sorts of random beliefs about luck. But Dad's ideas were always positive—always ways to improve one's fortune without having such a heavy focus on catastrophe. He said negative beliefs just sparked new fears, whether they were warranted or not.

A pang hit my heart with a familiar fierceness. I missed Dad so much. I missed the way he always put a bright spin on things, like suggesting the name Wink for my one-eyed puppy. The only other person I knew who could still lift my spirits that way was Cooper. I missed Cooper, too.

I balled the sock in my fist and decided I'd meet him at the tree house that night one way or another. Whether or not he could truly help me, I really needed the boost that came from just being around him.

When Mom finally came home later that night, her curls were even more frizzed-out than mine. "I went outside to study on my break and got locked in the courtyard," she said. "I pounded on the door, but I guess no one heard me with all the thunder. By the time Dr. Sanders happened to walk by and let me in, I was soaked to the bone. And since I was also fifteen minutes past the end of my break, Mr. Keen made me stay an extra hour. Without pay."

"Can he do that?" I asked.

Mom shrugged. "I really need this job," she said, turning her back on me to warm a can of soup in a pan. By then, I'd let Petey have two more helpings of cheesy puffs, and I'd wolfed down a handful myself. Unfortunately, the airy snacks weren't enough to fill our growling stomachs. But I hadn't dared turn on the stove until Mom got home.

After dinner, Mom practically had to drag Petey into the tub—their nightly ritual. Once Mom and Petey were both in the bathroom, it was easy sneaking out.

Cooper lived three blocks away *if* I stuck to the sidewalk. Double that if I took dirt paths and grassy fields, which I always did.

The Fiddleman house backed right up to open space. They had a large, unfenced yard, in which Cooper's tree house sat like a watchtower in an ancient maple tree.

The sky above the tree house was clear, the storm having long passed. It stayed light out longer now that it was nearing spring, but the sun had already sunk behind the horizon.

Something about the setting sun made me sad. Maybe because I felt like night was closing in on the day the same way my bad luck was closing in on me. The Luck Test would most likely bring an end to what little warmth and light I was holding on to—things like Cooper and this tree house.

I'd been climbing the ladder for years, since long before I'd known it wasn't sensible for me to do so. And by the time I figured out that it was too dangerous, I was already too attached, too fond of the time I spent there with Cooper, to stop.

The tree house, tucked as it was among the maple leaves and cut off from everything else, had been one of the few places—much like my bedroom—where I truly felt happy and safe.

I paused as I lifted my foot to the first rung. How long since I'd been here? One month, maybe two? I used to come here daily. It hurt, in a hollow, aching sort of way, to think about it, so I tried not to as I clambered up the remaining rungs.

Cooper was waiting inside. A poorly wrapped present with a crooked bow sat on the floor of the tree house in front of him. "Surprise!" he shouted.

"Cooper," I said admonishingly, but at the same time, I was unable to hold back a smile. "My birthday's not until Friday."

"Couldn't wait." He shrugged and then nudged the box toward me.

I took a seat, cross-legged, on the wooden slats of the tree house so that I faced Cooper, the gift forming a bridge between us. I took a moment to absorb it all. The joy-filled memories I had of this place. Playing fort and rolling marble armies down the lines between the wooden slats.

Feeling like we were the luckiest two people in all of Fortune Falls.

My stomach turned over. "You didn't happen to run into Felicia on your way home today, did you?" I asked hesitantly, not sure I wanted to hear his answer.

"What? Nooo." Cooper shook his head. "Will you *please* open your present already?" He flashed me a grin—crooked, just like the bow.

I beamed back at him and turned my attention to his gift. The box was much longer than it was tall, and I took my time sliding my fingers between the rippled tape and crinkled blue-and-white-striped paper. Then I gently lifted at the corners as I tried not to let hope trickle in. The box was too large to hold a four-leaf clover or a lucky rabbit's foot—not that I could even accept gifts as rare and valuable as those if he'd somehow managed to find them.

"Dying here," Cooper said. "And it's a slow, painful death."

I rolled my eyes and tore the wrapping off in one fell swoop.

"Do you like it?"

I stared down, somewhat baffled by the instrument behind the clear plastic cover. "It's a . . . telescope?"

Cooper opened the end of the box closest to him and slid the telescope out, letting the package fall to the floor along with the wrapping paper. "So you can see the stars. We'll put it in your room, and then you'll be able to wish on a star every night."

It was a nice thought, but . . . "The wishes only come true if you're the first person—" I cut myself off, suddenly understanding why Cooper had been so eager to give me the gift.

Unable to contain his excitement, he leapt to his feet and finished my sentence for me. "To see a star at night, I know. It's always a Lucky that sees it but . . . who knows, maybe with a little help from this telescope?"

As he hovered above me, it hit me how much the telescope must've cost. Not as much as a four-leaf clover or lucky horse-shoe, but still a great deal more than I thought he could afford—it wasn't like his family had any luck or money to spare. I suspected the only reason he passed his Luck Test was because he'd been able to use his birthday wish for it when he turned twelve last fall.

"I can't," I said, dropping my gaze to the floor and then peeking back up at him with my chin still tilted down. "You should keep it for yourself. Here in the tree house, you'll have a better chance than I will of getting the nightly wish anyway."

"But none of that matters. Not if I can't hang out with you. Not if you don't pass the Luck Test," he said softly, but his eyes were intense—as bright as the stars themselves.

His words hung heavy in the small space inside the tree house. I shifted my weight to one side and then the other. How could words that were so kind cause such a terrible ache in my heart?

Who knew? Maybe with the telescope, I could beat the odds. *Maybe.* Nightly wishes weren't as powerful as birthday wishes, but as Mrs. Swinton was fond of reminding her Undetermined students, "You never know. The smallest thing might just jump-start your luck."

Regardless, I felt so happy to be back in the tree house with my friend and so grateful for the thoughtful gift that I couldn't contain myself any longer.

I sprang to my feet and hurled myself at Cooper the same way Petey had earlier. Cooper moved the telescope aside to receive my hug, but I was forging forward too quickly, too carelessly. I knocked the telescope from his hands.

The unbalanced silver tube wobbled in the air, and we both dove and fumbled to catch it. But it was a tricky bird, slick and not wanting to be caught. The telescope crashed to the tree house floor with a clatter.

Cooper and I stared down at it in silent horror.

I'd done it again. I'd broken something Cooper had probably spent months saving up for. And with it, I'd shattered whatever short-lived hope we'd had for mending my luck. I didn't know what to say.

Cooper also seemed to be at a loss for words, but after a long moment, he said, "No. It's okay. Look, it's just the lens. It can probably be fixed." However, as he picked it up, careful to avoid the shards of glass, a rattle echoed from somewhere deep inside the hull of the telescope. He peered through the open end where the glass lens had been, and gasped.

"What?"

Cooper lowered the telescope. The skin on the back of my neck prickled when I saw the look on his face.

"What?" I asked a second time. I knew it had to be bad. It had to be something far worse than a cracked lens for him to be stalling this way.

"I'm *so* sorry, Sadie. I never would have bought it for you if I'd known . . ."

Fear and desperation crept into my voice in a way that made me sound whiny. I didn't like it, but I also couldn't help myself. "Known what, Cooper? Just tell me, please," I pleaded.

"Sadie, there was a mirror inside . . . probably to reflect the light . . . and . . ." He was still stalling, but I knew.

"It's broken."

6

LIGHTNING STRIKES

My knees buckled, and I struggled for air as panic truly set in. I'd broken a mirror. Seven years of bad luck. It would be a hefty, suffocating curse for someone with halfway decent luck. For someone like me, it was practically a death sentence. As the tingle at the base of my neck spread across my skin and my heart pounded in my ears, I thought, *I'll never pass the test now. I may not even live to take it.*

The dark sky rumbled with deep, unsettling rolls of thunder as I slid down the ladder, hardly bothering with the rungs, and staggered onto the grass.

"Sadie!" Cooper called after me. "Wait!"

Wait? I couldn't wait. I couldn't be anywhere near him. Whatever dark force I'd summoned with my mishap, had drawn back the storm. I knew it would bowl right through Cooper just to get to me. *Run!* My head screamed louder than Cooper and louder than the thunder. *Run! Sadie, run!*

I felt the hair on my arms lifting to stand on end, and I turned my eyes to the heavens, fully expecting lightning to strike me down. As I sprinted across his lawn and into the grassy field behind it, I tried to think of nothing else but putting distance between myself and Cooper. Fallen twigs and bramble clawed at my legs as I ran.

A flash of light illuminated everything around me. Then *boom*. The earth rattled, and the sound of thunder echoed in my ears. Even when I heard crackling and smelled smoke, I didn't stop running. Squatting down and tucking your head between your knees only works if the lightning isn't actually aiming for you. I did stick to the lower ground, however, and I avoided the taller trees and, of course, the stream.

I didn't truly believe I'd make it home alive, but somehow I did. Sneaking back in seemed pointless, so I crashed through the front door and slammed it shut behind me. Then I darted through the house, sliding curtains closed and unplugging all the electrical cords as I went. One advantage of not having a lot of money—there weren't that many things to unplug.

My mom stepped out of Petey's room seeming addled and more than a little bit afraid as she said my name: "Sadie. What's going on?"

Just then a clap of thunder rattled the windows and sent a tremor of vibration through the house. A loud whine came from the bathtub. Bathrooms aren't actually the safest places during electrical storms, but just try telling that to Wink.

I opened my mouth to speak but then closed it again, not sure how much I should tell her. Knowing would just fill her with dread, and like me, she had a big test coming soon. She was one exam away from her nursing degree. She didn't need any added distractions. Besides, there wasn't anything she could do about the mirror I'd broken.

"Mom? Sadie?" Petey called from his bedroom.

"Just a minute," Mom called back. Her eyes were coming into focus, and she was staring at me like she knew there was something weird about this storm. She just wasn't sure what.

"It's okay. You should go check on him," I said, and then thought to myself, *I shouldn't*.

I bolted for the stairs before she could fire off any questions about where I'd been and why the storm seemed to be knocking at our door, stalking her only daughter—at least, that's what it felt like to me.

It was a childish thing to do, but I ran straight for my bed and pulled my covers up over my head, waiting for the storm to die down. I lay in wide-eyed silence, quivering with each new flash of light, quaking with the thunderous clap that always followed. I lay there for what seemed like an eternity. But, eventually, the flashes became less and less frequent, and then ended altogether. *Like a beast, it has finally fallen asleep*, I thought.

Just to be certain, I waited another five minutes after the last angry boom to peek my head out from under the covers. The danger seemed to have passed for the moment, but if there was one thing I knew, it was that bad luck didn't ever just go away. And it wouldn't sleep for long.

It might wait and fester, but it never forgot to come for you once it'd been stirred. In Fortune Falls, no inauspicious act went unpunished, from a stroll under a ladder to accidentally opening an umbrella indoors. The broken mirror could mean seven years of bad luck throwing hard, haphazard punches, or it might just decide to deal me a knockout blow tomorrow. I had no way of knowing. No crystal ball.

What I did know was that I was more of a threat to the people around me than ever. I recalled another story I'd heard about a teenage girl who'd broken a mirror. Her entire family had been sucked into a sinkhole. Mere hours after she'd thrown and consequently shattered a contraband compact mirror at school (after breaking up with the slimy boyfriend who'd given it to her), they were all dead.

Mom and Petey were upstairs. What if the earth decided to open up and devour them right along with me? My heart twisted inside my chest. I had to get out.

I slid down and dug my school bag from underneath the

bed. I dumped out my red homework folder, a few pencils, a textbook, and an eraser. Then I ran to my dresser. As quickly as I could, I crammed in jeans, T-shirts, socks, and clean underwear. I paused at the ballet shoes strung over a knob. It wasn't like I even danced anymore, so what good would they do me?

What good had they ever done me? My father had insisted on enrolling me in ballet school shortly after my fourth birthday, even though we couldn't afford the lessons. He said it would improve my balance. Fewer stumbles. Fewer disasters. He drove me to every class and patched the rips in my leotard before each recital. At the same time, my mom enrolled in nursing school.

Dad had desperately been looking for ways to prevent accidents. And Mom, for her part, had decided on a career that would teach her how to treat the bumps, bruises, and broken bones she knew couldn't be avoided. For all their good intentions, neither one of them could help me now.

Scurrying up to the kitchen, I tossed in two of the three remaining apples and the half-eaten bag of cheesy puffs. I was sure Petey would want me to have them if he knew I'd be on my own. Then I quietly crept out the front door.

I just stood there for a minute, my heart thudding, my pulse racing, wondering, *What now?* It's not like I could leave Fortune Falls. Unluckies gave up on trying long ago—tires always blew at the edge of town, people suffered strokes and heart attacks just as they were about to cross over city limits—like bad luck, there was no escaping it. Even people with mediocre luck didn't want to risk it. As for the Luckies, they could probably leave, but why would they want to?

I glanced up. The sky was pitch-black overhead. No stars meant heavy clouds, but I didn't see any spindly fingers of lightning, either. Even if I didn't know where I was headed, I needed to get as far as possible from the people I cared about while I still had the chance.

I took one step and then another. I made it almost to the end of the drive before I noticed a small dark form sitting there. Waiting.

It took a second for my mind to register what I was seeing—a scraggly creature with short pointy ears and yellow eyes, surveying me with a steady gaze. A cat! Cats weren't allowed in Fortune Falls anymore. Not any, let alone this one with fur the color of ravens.

At one time, people had been allowed to keep cats as pets, but every now and then, someone would harbor a darkly colored kitten instead of turning it in for disposal. After too much heartache, too many deaths caused by crossing a black cat's path, all cats were banned. Now, like bunnies, they're extremely rare in Fortune Falls, but for an entirely different reason.

I had a personal vendetta against black cats. *If only they'd all been eliminated, then maybe . . .* But I couldn't stop to think about that. I didn't have time, and the memory was too painful. Instead, I glared and stomped my foot, but the cat refused to move on, refused to drop her yellow gaze.

A tremble ran down my spine and bile rose in my throat. I couldn't possibly pass her. Break a mirror and then cross a black cat's path all in the same night? That would certainly be the final nail in the coffin. So, instead of moving forward, I swallowed the bile and summoned the courage to scream, "What do you want, cat? Scram! Get out of here!"

But the cat wouldn't leave. She merely lifted a paw to her mouth and began smoothing the fur on it with her triangular pink tongue.

I tried to wait her out, thinking that when the vile creature was done grooming, she'd scurry on down the street. But she didn't. She just turned her uncanny eyes back toward me, and she didn't even flinch when the clouds overhead started up again with more angry grumbles.

By then, the blood-pulsing and adrenaline-driven urge to run away was starting to wane. My desire to protect my family wasn't, but it was being overshadowed by the impossibility of it. I had nowhere to run and obstacles like this black cat would most likely be waiting for me around each and every corner.

What could I do but surrender?

Miserably, I turned and retreated back inside. My arms hung limply at my sides as I lumbered down the empty hallway. No one seemed to have noticed I'd been missing. No doors creaked open. No heads poked out.

"Wink?" I whispered in the dark, hoping to hear the thud of her paws on the hardwood floor, but apparently she was still traumatized by the storm and was planning to spend the entire night in the bathtub.

Alone and with spirits so low, I didn't think they could drop any further, I returned to my room. I flipped on the light switch and crawled back under the sheets, fully clothed. Eventually, even with the light on overhead, I somehow drifted off to sleep.

7

CAT AND MOUSE

I carried the weight of my nightmares with me as I rose from bed the next morning. I guess the important part is that I did rise. When I'd fallen asleep the night before, I'd certainly had my doubts.

Light was reflecting off the aluminum window well when I awoke, and I walked over to the glass, angling myself to peer up and around the well at the sky above. Not a single cloud sullied the smooth pinkish-gray dawn.

If I had found a single thundercloud, I probably would've slunk right back into bed. But the peaceful, blush-colored tint of this clear-skied morning made me think that perhaps all was not lost.

The broken mirror felt no more real than the nightmares that had kept me tossing and turning all night. I could shrug the whole thing off, because it hadn't actually happened. Couldn't possibly have been true, or I wouldn't have been waking up like this—like it was any other morning.

Deep down, I knew it hadn't been a nightmare, of course. I knew that the curse I'd brought upon myself hadn't really dissipated with the light of a new day and that it wouldn't for seven more years. But pretending felt like hiding inside a protective shell. I didn't want to stop.

I glanced at the alarm clock. I'd overslept. If I missed school, I'd have to face the wrath of my mother. She'd already given permission for Petey and me to stay home on Friday. Not because it was my birthday, but because it was the thirteenth and she thought we'd be safer if we didn't leave the house.

Plus, the sun was shining brightly—what could possibly go wrong?

I scrambled for my backpack and dumped out all the clothes and food I'd crammed in the night before. I shoved my school stuff back in. There wasn't time to change, so I charged upstairs thinking it was a good thing I'd slept in my clothes.

Since Mom didn't have to go on shift until later, she was driving Petey to Pot-of-Gold and I was able to take a more direct route to school. Even while pretending that my life wasn't a ticking bomb, I wasn't deluded enough to think I didn't need to watch out for cracks in the sidewalk.

With my head down, I noticed the puddle first. It wasn't confined to the gutter like the one the day before. This puddle engulfed the entire sidewalk in a spot where the cement dipped low.

I was wondering how best to get around it when I heard a snap and looked up. The tree above me was charred and split down the middle. I reasoned that it had been struck by lightning during the previous night's storm. The crack I'd heard came from a heavy branch that had fallen on an electrical wire. It was now stretching the wire tight.

While I was still looking up, the limb snapped again and, this time, it splintered entirely away from the trunk, dragging the hot wire down with it. The wire skimmed across the puddle just a few feet in front of me.

I stood frozen, just shy of where the sparks flew and the air popped and sizzled. I wasn't actually shocked—unless you want to count the jolt the whole thing gave my heart—but I came very close to being electrocuted.

Thanks to my dad, I knew if only one of my feet was touching the ground, electricity could travel up one leg and down the other, my body acting as a channel for it to follow. So even though instinct told me to jump, I kept both feet on the ground and shuffled off the sidewalk and onto the road—better to risk being run over than being jolted by a live electrical wire. Once I was in the clear, I hurried past and continued on my way to school.

The near electrocution had definitely shaken me out of my stupor. So much for pretending the curse wasn't real. But, weirdly, I wasn't devastated by the wake-up call. I could only think that my dad would've been proud. I'd stayed calm, kept my wits about me, and remembered what to do. I'd just dodged a deadly strike.

Then I thought about the black cat I'd seen the night before. I remembered cats sometimes toy with their prey before going for the jugular. They'll toss mice in the air, cuff birds with their paws, or even let squirrels go, only to draw the critters back in for the fatal pounce.

But as I walked on, I decided that if Fate was determined to toy with me, I just had to keep dodging. Then, when an opportunity to slip beyond its reach came, I couldn't miss it. And, the way I saw it, my only opportunity would present itself in a few short days in the form of a birthday wish.

I actually made it to school on time, but the relief that came with that one tiny success didn't last very long. When Mrs. Swinton asked us to turn in our homework, I opened my backpack only to discover that I'd overlooked my red folder when I was shoving my school stuff back in. My paper on the original thirteen colonies was at home, most likely somewhere beneath my bed.

"You can stay in for lunch and recess and work on it then," Mrs. Swinton said, which actually wasn't so bad since I'd also forgotten my lunch and accidents were more likely to happen on the playground anyway.

As I rewrote my report for the third time (third time's a charm!), Mrs. Swinton said, "Have you had a chance to study for the spelling bee yet?"

While I'd been scribbling away about Jamestown, Virginia, the first permanent colony, she'd been sitting at her desk, eating black-eyed peas from a thermos and grading papers.

I groaned. The spelling bee? No, the spelling bee had been the furthest thing from my mind for the past twenty-four hours. "I don't think me being in the spelling bee is such a good idea, Mrs. Swinton," I said, lifting my head up from my report. "You might want to pick someone else." My heart sank a little as I said it. I hadn't been admitting it to myself, but there was a part of me that wanted to stay in the bee—if for no other reason than to aggravate Felicia.

"Nonsense," she replied, going back to making quick, sharp red marks on someone's paper. "You're the best speller in the class."

"But my luck!" I retorted.

Mrs. Swinton didn't even look up. "Haven't you ever heard that success begets success? Perhaps this spelling bee is exactly what you need."

For a long time after, I just stared at the two lucky horseshoes on the whiteboard. Mrs. Swinton had drawn the second one earlier that morning. I had just six more days before the day of the Spring Luck Test, and just today and tomorrow to study for the bee. Did she actually think I had a shot at winning?

I was still sort of frozen as the other students filed into the classroom, many of them sweaty and out of breath from having been outside. The stench of unwashed socks and underwear as Simon Swift walked by reminded me that the boys' baseball team was on a winning streak.

A winning streak.

Win the spelling bee. Pass the Luck Test. Is that what Mrs. Swinton was trying to tell me?

I might have stayed lost in my thoughts forever if someone hadn't tapped me on the shoulder. Mrs. Swinton was conjugating verbs up at the whiteboard, and Nathan Small was passing me a note.

I took the note from Nathan, but it wasn't from him.

Meet me at the Wishing Well after school. —Betsy

My first thought was that it must be a trick. Betsy was Felicia's friend after all. But when I glanced in her direction, she met my eyes and her smile was kind. Genuine. I didn't think it was something she could fake. I nodded my head slowly. I wasn't sure what she wanted, or whether or not I actually wanted to meet up with her, but I did think the Wishing Well might be worth a visit.

8

THE WISHING WELL

The Wishing Well is Fortune Falls's oldest landmark. It sits in the middle of a grassy square surrounded by an old clock tower and other historical buildings—many of which have been turned into trendy boutiques where the Luckies all like to shop.

Betsy was reading the copper plaque next to the well when I arrived.

> *Toss a coin into this well,*
> *And to the water spirit tell,*
> *Your deepest wish or favorite spell.*
> *Fate favors those who luck befell.*

"Doesn't it make you angry?" Betsy asked without looking up from the plaque when I sidled up next to her. "Basically it's saying your wish won't come true unless you're already lucky. Fate only grants wishes to 'those who luck befell.'"

"I don't know," I said. "I'm not sure anyone gets their wishes from this well anymore. Not even the Lucky." It was true. Most people believed the water sprite or nymph that had once dwelled here had abandoned us and our wishes long ago.

"But here we are," Betsy said.

"Yeah, here we are." I think what we both meant was "Are we really this desperate?" And the answer was yes.

She fished two pennies from her pocket and held one out to me. "It's not lucky, but I thought . . ."

"Thanks," I said, taking it from her. I was too embarrassed to admit that my own pockets were empty, but not so proud that I'd reject the coin.

Betsy stared silently at the well for just a minute before closing her eyes and tossing her penny in. Then she looked at me.

I took a deep breath. *What to wish for?* The list was too long: to undo the curse, to keep my family safe, for Cooper's parents to let him hang out with me, to get my birthday wish, and to pass the Luck Test—it was too hard to choose. Finally I closed my eyes. *I wish to be lucky*, I thought, hoping that would cover it all, and tossed the penny.

I opened my eyes just in time to see the penny slide down the inside wall of the well and land on an uneven stone ledge. The coin was too far down to be retrieved but not far enough to reach the water sprite—assuming there was still one living at the bottom of the well. So much for coming here being a good idea.

"Rotten luck," Betsy murmured.

"I know."

"Sorry I don't have another one."

I shrugged. "That's okay. It probably wouldn't make any difference."

"You must be wondering why I wanted you to meet me here."

I looked straight at her and nodded.

"I heard you talking to Mrs. Swinton about dropping out of the spelling bee. I think you should stay in it."

"Why?" I asked. Though what I meant was "Why do you care?"

"Because you should. Because you're a terrific speller. Because Felicia found a copy of the spelling list before we took the qualifying quiz and studied all the words ahead of time. Because someone needs to put her in her place. And because . . ." Betsy ended on a triumphant note: "Because the last five spelling bee champions have all gone on to Flourish Academy!"

"I thought you and Felicia were friends," I answered, unmoved. Well, not entirely unmoved. The part about the champions going to Flourish might've piqued my interest, but who's to say they weren't already Lucky to begin with.

"We are. We were. I don't know, okay? Yesterday I asked her if she'd let me borrow one of her charms for the Luck Test . . . She'd just found a lucky penny, her second one that day . . . And I've been to her house. She has like a gazillion lucky things. It's not like letting me borrow one for a day would be a big deal."

"Uh-huh," I said, remembering Felicia's grating squeal when she'd picked up the second shiny coin and the date with Cooper she'd thought it'd bring her. It must've been after I'd seen them pass the cemetery gates that Betsy asked Felicia to lend her a charm. "Let me guess. She said no."

"She said she'd love to help me out, but then I'd 'never learn to depend on my own luck and not be wasteful,' and then she told Sabrina that she shouldn't let me borrow one of her charms, either. I think she *wants* me to go to Bane's."

"So you want me to stay in the spelling bee, because you think I can beat Felicia." It felt strange to be having this conversation with Betsy, but it was nice to know that she thought I could win. "And you want to see her lose at something for once, because she's awful."

Betsy scrunched up her nose. "Yes," she admitted. "Does that make me just as awful as she is?"

"Not really." I couldn't imagine Felicia ever giving someone else a coin to toss into the Wishing Well. "But why did you ask to borrow a charm? Why didn't you just use your birthday wish?" The moment it slipped out I regretted it. It was kind of a personal question, and Betsy and I really didn't know each other that well.

She didn't seem angry with me for asking, but she did seem deflated. I almost said I was sorry, but then she blurted out, "My brother. I used it on my brother."

"You used your wish on your brother," I said, no less confused than before. I knew she had an older brother, but that's all I knew about her family. That, and that I'd never thought of any of them as *being unlucky*.

"Yeah. *One* bad choice and he wound up at Bane's instead of Flourish, and now I'll probably end up at Bane's, too." Betsy went very still and closed her eyes again. I think she was trying to hold back the flood of whatever emotions she was feeling.

I waited quietly to see if she'd say more, and sure enough, a long moment later, Betsy reopened her eyes and breathed in deeply through her freckled nose. She seemed a bit more composed and ready to tell her story. "He turned thirteen a few days ago . . . I thought there was a good chance he wouldn't survive the day if I didn't wish for it on my birthday. My birthday was just last week," she explained. "We were born almost exactly a year apart . . . Anyway, not all the kids who go to Bane's live past their thirteenth birthdays, you know. It's one reason Bane's is so . . ."

"Terrifying," I offered.

"I was going to say *safeguarded*. They have to be prepared for all types of disasters. But *terrifying* works, too."

We exchanged fleeting smiles.

"Our parents won't forgive him for not using his twelfth-birthday wish to pass the Luck Test. They say he threw his life away. And it's all because he wanted to be better at playing the guitar without actually having to practice. I guess he thought he had enough luck to pass the test without his wish. But he was wrong. He's crazy good now, but he can't even play it at Bane's. They wouldn't let him bring his guitar with him—something about the strings being too dangerous."

At some point while she was talking, Betsy had turned back to the well and was staring deep inside the black hole. She laughed coldheartedly. "Mom and Dad think I used my wish for the Luck Test. They're absolutely going to freak when they find out I threw away my future for him. They'll probably disown us both."

I wasn't sure what to say, so I just stood there until she finally tore her attention away from the well and turned back to me. "Do the spelling bee, Sadie. It may not seem like you have much of a chance, but any chance is better than none."

*   *   *

It's strange, I thought as I walked home alone, Betsy actually seemed to believe that hers was a lost cause and that mine wasn't—that the spelling bee could somehow be my lucky break. I wondered if she would've felt differently if I'd told her about the broken mirror.

Why hadn't I? Maybe because having someone believe in me made me feel like I could actually believe in myself.

I had survived the storm last night and the downed electrical wire this morning. I was already committed to dodging Fate's blows, maybe I could incorporate the spelling bee into my plans. Maybe I really could get a winning streak rolling with it. Win the spelling bee. Make my birthday wish. Pass the Luck Test.

Win spelling bee. Make birthday wish. Pass Luck Test. It sounded so simple when I broke it down.

I hurried home with an unfamiliar vigor, darting over the cracks in the sidewalk with a bold spring before bursting through the front door. There must've been a gleam in my eye as well, a light Mom hadn't seen in a while, because she seemed taken aback.

"What's gotten into you?" she asked, a smile blossoming on her face. She didn't even ask where I'd been. "You seem so chipper!"

My mom had the sleepy, half-open blue-green eyes of a dreamer. Staring at her, all I could do was smile back and pretend that my heart really was leaping. That I'd found the cheerfulness she so badly craved for me, for all of us—even though in actuality my energy was spurred more by grit than happiness.

"I qualified for the school spelling bee," I told her, "and I'm anxious for my birthday to come."

"Oh, Sadie. I'm so proud of you!" All the pretending was worth it to see her smile reach full bloom. "And that reminds me. I've been meaning to ask you what kind of ice-cream cake you want. Cookie dough, pistachio cream, Neapolitan?"

"Pistachio," I said. It wasn't my favorite, but I knew it was hers.

"Fantastic! I'll stop by the Dairy Freeze after work tomorrow and place an order. Petey and I picked up fresh apples at the store on our way home. And now I'm off to my room to study. Unless you need anything?" Mom had her back to me and was already walking down the hall.

"No," I answered. "I'll probably study for the bee and then take Wink for a walk."

"Sounds good, Sadie," Mom said.

I retrieved an apple from the kitchen and took a bite. Granny Smith this time, and the tartness made me pucker.

Then I sat down at the kitchen table and opened the study booklet Mrs. Swinton had given both Felicia and me.

"Tips and Tricks for Spelling Bee Success," the first page read. I imagined Felicia taking one glance at the booklet and immediately tossing the entire thing in the trash. When had she ever needed tips and tricks? Me, on the other hand . . . tips and tricks were how I survived.

I learned that an *s* and *c* were often used for the *s* sound in words that came from Latin. Words like *susceptible* and *visceral*. I read about words that came from Arabic and Asian languages, too. I'd never given much thought to where the words I used came from, but just reading about them made my world seem bigger somehow. Words that came from French and German and even ancient Greek had been floating around in my thoughts and connecting me with other people without me even knowing. That felt a bit like magic, and it made me sad to think I might not be able to compete at districts even if I won the bee.

When my eyes burned from staring at the booklet too long, I called to Wink. She came a thudding into the kitchen and then nuzzled my leg with her nose.

As I stood from the table, she excitedly pushed against my thigh. "Okay, okay," I said. She seemed to have a sixth sense about walks, always knowing when I was about to take her for one without me having to tell her. Now that I'd devoted a decent chunk of time to the first thing on my list, it was time to move on to the second.

Win the spelling bee. Make my birthday wish. Pass the Luck Test.

So what if Felicia never lost at anything? If I studied hard enough, it was bound to pay off. And so what if I'd never blown out all my birthday candles . . . not even once.

Last year, Dad's funeral had fallen on my birthday, and no one felt up for cake. The year before that I was in the hospital with pneumonia. When Wink was a puppy, she'd tugged the tablecloth and pulled the cake and all the candles down with it. There were a few years I'd come close, but time after time, there'd been candles left flickering.

My memories almost dragged me down, almost extinguished my drive entirely, but then Wink nudged me with her nose again and the flame rekindled.

No, I absolutely couldn't bear to be torn from her, and everyone and everything that mattered to me. This year, I was going to blow them all out. And for me to blow out all twelve candles with one single breath, my lungs definitely had to be in tip-top shape. Wink and I weren't going to walk, we were going to run.

9

HOLD YOUR BREATH

Before we left the house, I just had to do something about the ringlets falling into my eyes. I couldn't have anything interfering with my vision if I was going to up my speed.

Wink followed me to the bathroom, cocking her head to one side as I stepped up to the vanity and dug out a hair tie and a comb. On the very first swipe, the comb caught in my curls, flung out of my hand, and then slid through a crack in the vent cover on the floor.

It was bad enough that dropping a comb was a sign of a coming disappointment. But when I removed the vent cover, the shaft was too narrow for me to retrieve the comb, so I had to enlist the help of my little brother. Petey stuck his small hand down the shaft, retrieved the comb, handed it to me, and then scurried back to his building blocks after I thanked him for it. No problems whatsoever. The ease and simplicity of it sent a pang to my heart. To slide through life with barely a hang-up, rarely a scrapped knee, scarcely a nuisance—oh, to be a Lucky.

Would passing the Luck Test actually make me one? Was it still possible, even with the seven-year curse? I had to think that it was.

Wink barked to remind me that she was still waiting, and I patted her head. "One more minute, girl."

I put the comb back in the drawer and used just my hands to secure my hair in a messy ponytail. Then I bustled out the door as soon as I had Wink attached to her leash.

Standing on the front porch, I considered my options. I thought about running behind the neighborhood and through the greenbelt behind the Fiddleman house, but I knew if I ran into Cooper, he'd want to talk. Because I'd stayed in for lunch and recess to redo my homework, he hadn't had a chance to broach the subject of the broken mirror. And I didn't really want to give him one.

I glanced down at Wink. Her tongue was hanging out of her mouth, and she was staring at me expectantly with her one good eye. Understandably, her patience seemed to be wearing thin.

"We'll stick to newly paved streets, staying close to the gutter. No cracks, no risk, right?" Wink panted in agreement.

As soon as I broke into a light trot, Wink dug her paws

into the pavement, pulling hard on the leash. She outpaced my every step. "Whoa, Wink," I said. She turned her head to look at me, and her eye was so full of joy this time, I felt bad for holding her back.

Between our small, fenced backyard and my never-ending caution, Wink rarely had the opportunity to run. My lungs were starting to burn and my muscles felt tight, but even if I'd wanted to, I couldn't stop now.

Wink barreled forward, so I pumped my feet faster, and for just a moment, I experienced some of her joy. The feeling of letting everything go and not caring. The feeling of just being free. My chest expanded, and my legs felt powerful. I could run forever. Blowing out twelve candles would be simple. How could it not be? I would have my wish, and nothing would be beyond my reach.

I met Cooper on the road just as I rounded the first bend. His face went from thunderclouds to sunshine the instant he saw me. "Sadie!" he said. "There you are!"

"Oh, hey," I said, barely slowing my feet, thinking I could brush him off and keep on jogging. And I would have, too, if Wink hadn't betrayed me. She pulled on the brakes and wouldn't budge as she launched a playful, licking attack on Cooper.

My best friend counterattacked with a scratch behind Wink's right ear. Truly, it wasn't a fair fight. Wink was forced to surrender as her back foot starting thrumming uncontrollably.

Cooper laughed when Wink's good eye nearly rolled back into her head with pure bliss, and I couldn't help but smile. I wasn't pretending anymore. My best friend's laughter and the jogging had made me feel light and cheerful. Plus, the sky was clear, like it had never known a stormy day. I just wanted to freeze that moment and live it forever.

But then Cooper sobered up, and the hasty way in which his face switched from laughter to grim sobered me up, too. "I've been looking for you since school let out. That broken mirror . . ." he said. "What are we going to do, Sadie?"

I opened my mouth to tell him about my winning streak plan, but there was something about the concern in his eyes that made it all feel a bit foolish. I fell silent.

Cooper stopped scratching behind Wink's ear, then lurched forward and wrapped me in a hug. It was sudden and snug, and more than a little awkward. I breathed in his boyish smell—hand soap mixed with dirt—and felt myself tense beneath his arms. We weren't usually the hugging sort of friends.

He pulled back when Wink got jealous and butted her nose in between us. Cooper started laughing again. It was a softer chuckle this time but enough to break the tension.

"Sorry, Wink," he said. "I've just been really worried about

Sadie." He caught my eye when he said this, and I felt myself blush. I looked away hoping he wouldn't notice.

"Can we talk? Please, Sadie. We can figure something out. I know we can," he pleaded.

There was a park nearby. I sighed, walked over to a post near the entrance, and looped the end of Wink's leash around it. My hands felt sweaty, so I wiped them on my pants. "The swings?" I asked.

Cooper nodded.

The park wasn't crowded, and we each took an open swing. Not pushing off the ground but not sitting still, either, we swayed back and forth in silence for a few minutes.

"It's not fair. I'm not supposed to hang out with you *after* school. I barely get to see you *at* school. And next year . . ." Cooper's voice broke slightly, and I felt a shiver run through my body just at the thought of living at Bane's. "You have to pass the test, Sadie. You just have to."

"I know," I said solemnly.

"Maybe we can set a time and place to meet in secret each day, you know, to strategize. You have no idea how scared I was when you weren't at lunch, and then I went by your house again after school and you weren't there, either . . ."

"Cooper," I said, coming back to my senses. *He'd come by my house? It must've been while I was at the Wishing Well with Betsy.* "Maybe you shouldn't be looking for me at all. I—"

Just then a streak of black whizzed by, followed by the blur of Wink's lighter-colored fur as she went careening by as well.

"Wink!" I shouted, and bolted from the swing. "Don't!" But it was too late. She was charging after the black cat, and there was nothing I could say or do to stop her.

"Was that—?"

"Yeah," I said. My heart pounded in my chest as the two forms darted across the park, into prickly bushes, and squeezed out through the fence on the other side. I tore after them, and Cooper darted after me. I found a narrow opening in the shrubberies and burrowed my way through. Thorny stems dug into my skin as I went. When I reached the fence, I couldn't go any farther.

The cat and Wink must've managed to wriggle their way through a hole beneath the chain links—a hole I couldn't fit through. I glanced up, looking for another way, and felt like Fate was taunting me: "Come on, Sadie, test your luck. Just see if you can climb it." No, I couldn't. It was too high. A fall would cause serious injury, and I could hardly continue the chase with a broken leg.

My best option was to backtrack until I could work my way around the fence. Cooper, on the other hand, had already scrambled halfway up the chain links. *Please don't get hurt because of Wink, because of me*, I thought as I wove my way back through the bushes.

I was fuming by then, and tiny droplets of blood were trickling down my arms and legs where thorns had punctured my skin. How could I be so unlucky, or worse, so careless?

When I reached the post, I could see that Wink's leash was still attached to it. She must've somehow pulled free where it had clipped to her collar. Why hadn't I double-checked?

I had to live my life expecting things to always break and go wrong. But I'd slipped up, and Fate had swooped in again to knock me down.

No, I wasn't quite knocked down yet.

I ran as fast as I could back through the entrance and caught up with Cooper. He was shouting for Wink at the top of his lungs, and I added my voice to his.

"She isn't coming. We need to go after her," I said when Wink didn't appear. Since neither of us had any clue which direction she'd gone, we opted to split up.

Cooper went left and I went right, and it wasn't long before I thought I heard faint barking in the distance. Following the clamor, I cut across lawns and jumped over short picket fences. Avoiding the sidewalks, I aimed for as direct a path as possible. Then I heard a loud crash, and a trash can came rolling out of an alley right in front of me. Suddenly the two were back in sight. The collision had slowed them down, but only by a little.

I hurdled over the can. "Wink!" I called again. She glanced back at me but refused to give up the chase. The excitement gleaming in her eye and her tongue flapping in the wind told me she was having way too much fun.

If only I could say the same. On the upside, my chest was aching again. This pursuit had to be doing wonders for my lung capacity. I lost count of how many blocks we'd run, but at last, I was gaining on Wink. She was only about an arm's length away, close enough I thought I could dive-tackle her in just a few more steps.

I was so absorbed with catching Wink that I didn't notice where we were. That was until I recognized the fallen iron gate and immediately slid to a halt. Since my breath was already stuck in my throat, I didn't even have to suck it in.

I swear I heard the black cat purr as she easily vaulted the gate, and Wink bounded in after her. *NO!* I screamed inside my head. *No, no, no!*

The cemetery was huge, and within seconds, Wink disappeared from sight again. I backed up a few shaky steps and released the air trapped inside my chest. *What was I going to do?* My legs continued to tremble as I paced back and forth in front of the cemetery entrance, calling Wink's name over and over again until I was blue in the face.

I thought about holding my breath and going in, but there was no way I could hold it long enough to fetch Wink and make it safely back outside. My eyes stung as hot tears pooled in the corners. Then a howl followed by a hiss rang out deep inside the graveyard. I ran to the fence, my cheeks puffed out with every last bit of air they could hold, and peered through the iron posts.

Where are you, where are you, where are you? I chanted in my head as I scanned the cemetery for any signs of movement. Would the otherworldly things that haunted the cemetery even bother with a dog? I'd never heard of any animals dying inside, but what if I was wrong?

The sun was lowering in the sky, so the shadows behind each of the grave markers were elongated and distorted. Winged marble angels cast beastly dark images on the far overgrown grass. Tangles of vines and bushes wrapped like ghastly, grasping fingers around the crosses.

I'd never dared to get this close. I hoped to never get this close again.

A small, dark shadow with an arched back scurried across the large mausoleum towering over a far corner of the cemetery. I stepped back gasping for air. Then, without thinking, I forged ahead, keeping my distance from the iron posts as I worked my way around the outside of the fence. I took the opportunity to call for Wink again—praying she'd hear me, abandon the cat, and come crawling back out into the open.

Prickly shrubs cut into my already bloodied calves. Barbed goat head thorns attached themselves to my socks. The area outside the cemetery was as unkempt as it was inside. The temperature was dropping along with the sun, and where my skin wasn't scraped it was pimpled by goose bumps. My clothes were damp with sweat, and the chill I felt in the cool breeze was bone-deep. Carrying on, I reached the spot just outside the mausoleum where I'd seen the black cat's shadow.

One, two, three, I counted. I sucked in another large gulp of air. Then I raced to press my face against the fence again. I saw nothing at first—just more downtrodden headstones and overgrown vines—until the black cat stepped out from behind a tall, angular grave marker.

It was the same scrawny thing I'd seen after breaking the mirror the night before. But now that she was standing, I could see that she didn't have a tail. Well, none to speak of anyway. The nub where her tail should've been was approximately two inches long. *Good*, I thought, *but I wish whatever took your tail had taken the rest of you with it!*

The cat just stared back at me with yellow eyes and an unwavering glare. She seemed to be mocking me. Barely older than a kitten, I knew it couldn't be the cat my father had seen over a year ago, but I hated her as if she were the very same.

"It was dark out," Dad had said the night before he died. "I couldn't tell whether the darn thing was black or just chocolate brown. Cats do come in chocolate brown, don't they?" I think he was trying to sound lighthearted, but he was unable to keep his voice from quavering with emotion.

I'd stood frozen behind the crack in the door at the top of the basement stairs. Dad had been hidden from view, but peering through, I'd been able to see Mom standing in the middle of the kitchen in her favorite threadbare lilac bathrobe. Perhaps it would've been better if I hadn't seen *her* face either—dread had weighed down every feature. Even her curls had hung limp.

"Henri, I . . . I . . ." My mom's voice had failed her. She choked on a sob.

"What was I supposed to do, Caroline?" Dad had said, rushing to her side, brushing a curl behind her ear, a thumb across her cheek. My mom leaned into him.

The sad, broken tenderness of it all caused me to avert my eyes in shame. It was a private moment, and I shouldn't have been spying. But what I heard my dad say next made my heart clench hard inside my chest. "I promised her."

Earlier that evening, I'd forgotten my ballet slippers at home. I'd broken into tears the moment I realized I didn't have them, and Dad had promised to retrieve the slippers while I was getting ready. Warming up barefooted, I'd tried to ignore Felicia's and Sabrina's snickering as they performed their flawless pirouettes within their perfect slippers.

As promised, Dad was back seconds before the recital started. His face had been ashen and beaded with sweat, but I'd hardly noticed. I'd merely slipped into my ballet shoes and ran onto the stage. I'd bumbled my way through the recital, and I never would've known that Dad had encountered the black cat if I hadn't overheard my parents talking.

The very next morning, Dad fell from a roof. Fate didn't toy with him. It went straight for the kill.

An added curse to being unlucky was having to take the more hazardous jobs, the jobs that lucky people could avoid. My dad was a roofer, but he had always been careful. Still, his safety-mindedness wasn't enough to counter the effects of having crossed a black cat's path.

When I returned to school after the funeral, my classmates were whispering behind my back. It seemed they all were speculating that he'd walked beneath one of his ladders.

My guilt had been too sharp to correct any of them. It hadn't been a ladder. It was the cat's fault, and Dad never would've crossed its path if I hadn't been crying over my dumb ballet slippers. I stopped dancing that day, and I'd hated cats with a vengeance ever since.

So, as the black cat stood staring back at me, still and watchful from inside the cemetery, I seethed. My insides boiled. I wanted to scream bloody murder at her, but I didn't dare open my mouth.

I willed myself to swallow my hate and clear my head as I frantically scanned the area. Wink *had* to be somewhere nearby. A black cat had cost me my dad. I couldn't let one cost me my dog, too.

I kept my ears peeled, but besides an occasional rustle of the wind blowing through leaves, the cemetery was eerily silent. Just as I was about to take a step back and replenish my air supply, something else caught my eye. To the left of the mausoleum and the black cat, and close to where I was standing by the fence, something was sticking out from the bushes. Slender, boney white fingers. A skeletal hand, reaching, stretching, grasping for the iron posts.

This was not the hand of someone who'd been buried in the cemetery. It was the boney remains of someone who'd thought they'd be able to dash in and out while holding their breath. Whoever it was had been wrong. Deadly wrong.

The black cat hissed a low sound that was both threatening and melancholy. I stumbled back from the fence and ran. It might've been that I was halfway home before I even realized I was running and found the courage to breathe again.

10

WISHBONE

Mom was sympathetic when I told her I'd lost Wink, but Petey refused to talk for the rest of the evening. He wouldn't look at me as we ate dinner, and he didn't even protest when Mom said it was time for his bath. I think he was hoping to find Wink waiting for him in the tub. Even though I'd retreated downstairs by then, I could hear his wails ringing through the house when he discovered that she wasn't.

I awoke the next morning to an unnervingly empty house, and it caused a powerful wave of grief and loneliness to course through me. On days like this, when Mom and Petey left before I even got up for school, Wink had always been there to lick my face if I was feeling sluggish. Even if she stayed upstairs while I got ready, I could hear her paws pounding on the kitchen floor above me. The silence made me feel more alone than I'd ever felt in my life.

I wasn't scared. I just felt dead. On the inside. I felt like never crawling out of bed again.

Then I remembered Dad taking me on a trip downtown after my broken collarbone had healed, but my spirits hadn't. "See these people," he'd said. "These are the luckless that have given up." We drove by windows that had been broken out with baseball bats, and sidewalks that were in some places shattered by sledgehammers and in other places overgrown with vines. On the streets were people with unkempt hair and beards and expressionless faces. The worst were those staring off into space as they sat immobile on curbs or behind blowing curtains.

"I know broken bones hurt, Sadie girl. So does embarrassment," Dad had said. "But I think what Fate really wants is to make you stop trying. That's its biggest success. Not ending your life, but making you feel dead while you're still alive."

So I got up.

With a lot less gusto than the day before, I repeated to myself: *Win spelling bee. Make birthday wish. Pass Luck Test.* Then I slowly walked to school and found my way to the classroom for Undetermined students.

Mrs. Swinton added a third horseshoe to the board—five more days before the Luck Test. Nathan was nervously gnawing on a pencil and appeared to have chewed halfway through it. Betsy's face quirked into a bittersweet smile when our eyes met, and I thought about the double meaning of the word *undetermined*. Sure it meant unknown, unidentified—as in, we hadn't yet been identified as Lucky or Unlucky. But it also meant hesitant, faltering, and unsure. Maybe the word actually did still fit a number of us.

By the middle of the day, it was hard to remember why I had chosen to get out of bed. Nothing too terrible happened, but even common nuisances—like my pencil box spilling on the floor—felt like more than I could handle. At least Betsy rushed to my side to help me clean up the mess.

At lunch, I didn't attempt to sit by anyone in the cafeteria—just found a spot alone at the end of one of the long Formica tables. When I glanced up, Betsy offered me another weak smile from across the room but then went back to chatting with a quiet girl from our class. It was the first time I'd ever seen her not eat with Sabrina and Felicia.

When the sixth-grade Luckies walked in, every eye turned to look. Never was there a more glossy-haired, gleaming-smile, pristinely dressed bunch. Laughing, giggling, and carrying on, the fortunate students found open tables and seats together at which to eat their fancy, well-packed lunches. One of the Luckies had won a drawing at the local pizzeria for a year's supply of their deep-dish pies. She was handing out freshly delivered slices of pepperoni to everyone sitting at her table.

Sabrina and Felicia hopped up from their seats and I assumed the girls were planning to join the Luckies eating pizza, so I was shocked when instead they sat down at the far end of my table. That was until I noticed how loudly they were talking. They obviously wanted me to hear their conversation.

"Guess who I ran into when the teacher sent me to the office for paper clips?" I didn't think Mrs. Swinton liked Felicia enough for her to be the teacher's pet, but she could be trusted to travel the hallways without causing any disturbances. Mrs. Swinton never sent me on any errands.

"Hmmm," Sabrina jested. "It wasn't a Lucky boy whose name begins with *C* and ends with *R*, was it?"

"It *was*. And as Cooper walked by me, I accidentally on purpose spilled the entire box." Felicia giggled. "Sadie's clumsiness gave me the idea," she said. "And when he stopped to help me pick up the paper clips, he totally brushed my hand. I know he meant to."

Felicia's eyes flitted toward me. I dropped my gaze an instant too late, catching her crafty smile. Satisfied I was listening, she kept talking loudly to Sabrina: "I'm going shopping for a new black dress after school today. Do you want to come?"

"What do you need a new dress for? Oh, I know . . ." Sabrina said, playing along.

"The Friday the Thirteenth Dance!" the two friends squealed in unison.

Just then a Lucky named Daniella was walking by. She leaned in and shouted, "Jinx!"

Instantly both girls were struck mute.

It was sort of hilarious watching them open their mouths and emulate speech without any noise coming out. I flashed Daniella a grateful smile. She smirked, found a place to sit with some other Luckies, and went about eating her lunch. I wondered how long she would let them go on like that before saying either of their names aloud.

School might be terrible, I thought to myself as I went back to my soggy peanut butter and raspberry jam sandwich, *but at least now it's quiet*.

Ten minutes into our lunchtime, Cooper plopped down in the empty seat across from me. I felt an instant boost. Even though I knew I should tell him to sit somewhere else (for his own good), I couldn't bring myself to do so. "Sorry I'm late," he said as though we had a standing lunch date. We didn't. "I had to ask Mr. Barton something after class." Mr. Barton was Cooper and the other Luckies' teacher.

As Cooper launched into an explanation, I peered out of the corner of my eye at Felicia. She was scowling at me and trading scornful looks with Sabrina. I wondered briefly if there was a way to jinx facial expressions. I would've given anything to put the two girls' faces on mute, right along with their voices.

"So do you want to give it a shot?" Cooper asked.

"Huh?"

"The wishbone. I know it's from a chicken, not a turkey, but Mr. Barton seemed to think it should have the same effect."

"Oh, right."

Cooper was holding a wishbone—from where?—his lunch, I guessed—out between us. I took hold of one of the sides. We pulled at the exact same time, and of course, it snapped in his favor. I realized as I held the shorter end in my hand that I hadn't even bothered making a wish as I pulled.

Cooper frowned. "I was trying not to put much pressure on it. I thought that way you'd have a good chance of getting your wish."

I could hear him speaking, but my mind was a million miles away. The thin bone I held between my fingers reminded me of the hand at the cemetery, and then all I could think about was Wink. I must've looked pretty crushed, because Cooper was falling all over himself apologizing. "I'm so sorry, Sadie. It was a stupid idea."

I shook my head. "It was a nice idea. I'm just worried about Wink."

"Didn't you catch her? When I circled back to the park, I ran into Felicia. I thought she might help us look for Wink, but when I asked, she said she'd just seen you walking home with her. I . . ." Cooper trailed off probably realizing that whatever Felicia had said had been a lie.

I shook my head, but just thinking about the graveyard had made me suck in my breath. I let it out. "Wink chased the cat into the old Fortune Falls Cemetery."

"The cemetery?" Cooper stiffened. "Not good. Not good at all." He eyed his longer end of the wishbone, and I knew what he was thinking. "If I would've known, I would've wished for her to come back. I wished—"

"Shh," I said. "Don't tell me or it won't come true."

"Okay. But I'm going to help you get her back. I promise." Cooper's dark brown eyes shined with determination.

I smiled. I had desperately needed a reminder of why it was important to keep fighting Fate, and here one was. Sitting right across from me.

"We just need a plan," Cooper said. "Say you'll meet me after school? Please, Sadie."

"Um," I stalled. "I don't know." I was anxious to get back to the cemetery to look for Wink again, but with my extra-horrendous luck, it was the last place I needed to drag Cooper.

The bell rang signaling the end of lunch, and he stood up. "Please?" he pleaded a second time.

Cooper always was better at formulating plans than I was. I usually talked myself out of things—just like I'd almost talked myself out of the spelling bee. I still hoped to use the bee to start a winning streak, but with Wink missing now, things were getting even more complicated. I knew I could use his help. Finally, I relented with a curt nod of my head. "But just to plan. We'll meet at the park."

"Yes!" Cooper said. "You got it!" He started to walk away, headed for the line of Luckies gathering near the entrance to the cafeteria, but he stopped after just a few feet. Flashing me a crooked grin, he took a step back in my direction and whispered secretively, "It appears my wish is already coming true."

11

LUCKY CHARMZ

Mom was picking Petey up again, so I went straight to the park after school let out. I waited by the swings, whipping my head around every time I heard a woof or the soft tinkling of dog tags. Of course, the barks and jingles all belonged to other people's dogs and not to Wink.

Cooper arrived five minutes after me, which I found suspicious. For one thing, he was far more daring than me and would've traversed the sidewalk cracks with greater speed. For another, the release time for the Luckies was fifteen minutes earlier than it was for everyone else. That way they could clear the school grounds long before the calamity-causing Unluckies were unleashed. Felicia's parents had secured special permission for her to leave school early each day, too.

He was jogging and out of breath. So much so that he had to rest his elbows on his knees before explaining where he'd been. "Sorry," he said.

I wished he'd stop apologizing. It wasn't his fault that my

dog was missing, or that the wishbone snapped in his favor, or that I'd broken the gift he'd given me for my birthday. If anything I should be the one apologizing for always bringing him down.

"Since I got out early, I ran by the cemetery. You know, just to check." He shook his head. "But I didn't find her."

I shot daggers at him with my eyes. "What were you thinking?" I asked angrily.

Cooper rarely got mad, but in that moment, his temper flared as hot as I'd ever seen it. With a tight mouth and clenched jaw, he said, "I was thinking that you are my friend. And friends help friends. I was also thinking that you're not the only one who cares about Wink. I want to find her as badly as you do."

"Oh," I said, and then, trying to smooth things over, I added, "Thanks. So what's the plan?"

Cooper melted, his anger gone as quickly as it had arrived. "First stop, Lucky CharmZ."

I balked. "Are you serious?" Lucky CharmZ was basically a black-market shop for all things luck-related. Unlike the boutiques where the uber-Luckies all shopped, it carried more than just the lucky charms its name implied. Danger-ously unlucky items were sold there as well.

Cooper shrugged. "Desperate times call for desperate measures. We need to know what we're up against here. If anyone knows how to best combat this unlucky streak, it's Zeta."

Dad had brought me to Lucky CharmZ a few times. Zeta had seemed more like a butcher than a storekeeper, and had a history as shady as the cemetery.

Cooper was probably right, though. Luck had so many nuances, so many rules to follow; it was difficult to keep them all straight. Talking to someone with real insight could only help.

"Okay," I said at last. "You're right."

Cooper grinned. "I usually am."

Lucky CharmZ was located in the same part of town my dad had driven me through years before. The area where the luckless who'd hit rock bottom lived. It was also where the graduates of Bane's would most likely end up someday.

Some of the windows were now boarded up with sheets of steel. Crows couldn't tap at broken-out glass, but a bird flying inside your house was every bit as devastating of an omen. On a good day, some of Fortune Falls's most destitute must've banded together to put up the barriers. Maybe Fate hadn't quite won its war with them yet.

"How was the rest of your day?" Cooper asked. He sensed I was nervous, and was trying to take my mind off our surroundings. Some of the windows may have been boarded up, but everything was still dilapidated—paint peeling, shutters falling down. Obviously, no one had dared pull out a ladder to fix anything in ages. But if Cooper was trying to distract me, this wasn't the question to ask.

I leveled him with a look. "Well, I'm still alive."

Cooper's eyes widened for a fraction of a second.

"Yours?" I asked. "How are things with the upper crust? What's it like being a *Lucky*?" The word *Lucky* came out sounding as bitter as it tasted on my tongue.

"They aren't that bad," he said quietly.

I noticed that he'd used the word *they* instead of *we*, but I didn't point it out.

Cooper went on. "It's just that when everything you've ever done turns out perfect and everything you've ever wished for came true, I think it changes you."

"I wouldn't know," I said, hoping he'd break into one of his impressions. Something like "No, Mommy, this pony is too tall. Let's return it for a shorter one."

Instead he said, "I think they get bored. It makes them say and do things that seem ridiculous to us. Nothing's a challenge, but it's almost like they want one, you know, because things are *too* easy. If you or I had been born under a supremely lucky star, the way they were, we probably would've turned out just like them."

Again, I almost reminded him that he'd already passed the test. For all intents and purposes, he *was* a Lucky. But I didn't want to. It felt good to have Cooper aligning himself with me rather than his classmates.

I wondered if that was one of the reasons Felicia was so interested in Cooper. Maybe she saw him as a challenge. He wasn't the most popular boy in school, and he was far from being the luckiest of the Luckies. But he was different. He couldn't care less about one's fortune (obviously, since he liked to hang out with me), and that made it harder for Felicia to use her charms on him. Yet, if Felicia got everything she ever wished for, then . . .

"We're here," Cooper announced.

I glanced up at the one freshly painted sign in this part of town. The *U* in *Lucky* was a horseshoe. It hung on the side of a giant warehouse made of sheet metal painted a bright blue color.

The shop owner was standing behind the counter when we walked in. He was wearing a black muscle shirt. It was hard not to notice his big, burly arms tattooed with images of four-leaf clovers and dream catchers, and a giant letter *Z* with a squiggly line after it on his bulging right shoulder.

Cooper whispered in my ear, "It's the symbol for Zeta. I have no idea if it's his real name or not, but Zeta has the value of seven in the system of Greek numerals—seven being a lucky number, of course." I raised a brow. My friend wasn't dumb, but he wasn't a scholar, either. "I asked him once," Cooper murmured in reply.

Around Zeta's beefy neck hung a necklace with an open palm and an eye in the center. I recognized it as a hamsa hand. The charm, if it was real, was supposed to be awesomely powerful for protection against evil. It was also insanely expensive and, without a doubt, incredibly difficult to get one's hands on in Fortune Falls.

Zeta saw me staring. He had an untamed, distrustful look, like a caged wild animal. Something told me he hadn't been born lucky. He'd taken his luck by force and wile. It probably caused him to sleep with one eye open at night, always expecting someone to sneak in and take back what he'd stolen. Or maybe mistrust and paranoia were just by-products of the trade.

"What do you kids want?" he asked in a voice that matched his gruff appearance.

"Hey, Zeta," Cooper said coolly, obviously less rattled than I felt. "Remember me? I bought a telescope from you last week."

Before he could respond, a baby pig, pink and plump, ran across the room. Zeta swooped down to pick her up, his face beaming with delight. "There she is! There's my girl." He started snuggling the pig and making little snorting noises.

He held the pig out for us to see. "Meet Chance," he said. "*Schwein haben.* It means 'to have a pig' in German, which is a very lucky thing." He kissed Chance directly on the snout and then set her down. She squealed appreciatively and scurried off behind the counter. Cooper and I shared a look.

"Now about that telescope, did I tell you or what? Bet your girlfriend is racking up the wishes."

"We're just friends," I blurted out at the same time Cooper said, "It broke."

"Broke, huh?" Zeta said. Then he went right back to being gruff as he pointed to a sign that read *No Handouts. No Refunds.*

Cooper ignored him. "We're here about the mirror inside the telescope—that's the broken part we're concerned about."

Zeta let out a puff of air. "Shame. But, you know, you get what you pay for. What'd you do with the pieces?"

"Buried them," Cooper said, which came as a surprise to me. I'd been too distraught after it happened to even think about what to do with the broken shards.

"Hmm. Okay, we're-just-friends girl, what's your constitution—providence-wise?" Zeta asked me.

"Not the best. Pretty awful, honestly," I answered.

"Hmm," Zeta said again. "Well, smart thinking, burying them." I flashed Cooper a grateful smile but wasn't able to say thank you since the store owner was still talking. "Not as good as rinsing them in a stream but, if you're lucky, possibly enough to save your life."

"I'm not lucky," I said. I thought I'd made that clear before, but I guess not.

"You're still here, aren't you?" Zeta shot back. "If you continue to hang on like this, you're in for a very rocky seven-year stretch, though. Too bad he's not your boyfriend." He nodded at Cooper. "Or else you might talk him into buying you a rabbit's foot."

"Is that what it would take?" Cooper asked. "A rabbit's foot?"

Zeta might as well have said the Hope diamond. Curse and all, I'd have about as much luck affording it. Glancing around the warehouse, I took in the patch of four-leaf clovers growing beneath a greenhouse light, the horseshoes hanging on the wall, the boxes of meteorite fragments and telescopes on one side of the counter, and bowls full of hand-carved bone dice, amber beads, and acorns on the other. All of it was way out of my price range. I didn't even have a price range.

"What about a winning streak that includes a birthday wish? Would that be enough?" I piped in. I felt Cooper's eyes on me, but I kept staring straight ahead. I hadn't mentioned my win-spelling-bee-make-birthday-wish-pass-Luck-Test plan to him yet.

"You're on a winning streak?" Zeta asked, obviously dubious.

"Not yet, but—"

"And you think you'll get your birthday wish?" he scoffed.

"I don't know. Look, I'm just asking."

Zeta shrugged his boulder-like, tattooed shoulders. "Maybe. It's a start anyway. All wishes have their limitations." I knew that already. Not even a Lucky could make a wish that wasn't bound by certain laws of the universe. You couldn't wish to fly or turn invisible, or to bring someone back from the dead. It had to be something relatively plausible.

"One wish probably isn't enough on its own, but if you use it right, you could probably wish your way into enough good luck to counteract the bad." The soft voice he'd used when talking to Chance was long gone. "Luck is consumable. Each charm has a certain amount to use up. Pennies will buy you one lucky day, but if you play your cards right, you don't waste the penny's luck wishing for a snow cone or kiss from your sweetheart . . ." He waggled thick black eyebrows sitting below a shiny bald head at us, before leaning in like he was letting us in on a secret. "Then, maybe, you can use the penny's charm to find a four-leaf clover. Then you use that four-leaf clover to find two more. And so on. It can take a while, but one lucky break and eventually you can build a fortress."

Zeta straightened up proudly. I really did wonder if he'd socked someone in the eye (or worse) for his first lucky break, or if perhaps he'd legitimately built his emporium of fortune by stumbling upon one heads-up penny.

"For seven years, though," the shop owner continued, "yeah, you'd have to build up to *at least* a rabbit's foot. Curse will probably have run its course by then—that is if burying the shards did the trick and you're still alive. Unless . . . you consider buying." He pointed to a row of furry severed feet inside a locked glass case, along with a few scarab amulets, and other exotic-looking charms and crystals. "These are the heavy hitters."

"With the price tags to match," Cooper said.

"Gotta feed my pig," Zeta shot back, quick as lightning.

"What about those?" I asked, tipping my head toward several items behind the counter.

Zeta eyed me suspiciously. "You into hexes and dark magic, we're-just-friends girl?"

"I . . . No," I faltered.

"Good," Zeta said. "That chair . . ." He pointed to an antique wooden rocker strung up with ropes, hanging from the ceiling behind the counter. "The original owner killed a man just for sitting in 'his chair,' and was hung for his crime. Now the chair is a death curse to anyone who sits in it. Not that people listen. That's why I hang it up.

"See those green stones, Blarney Stones. Lucky if you kiss them in Ireland. Totally opposite effect here. And the Maori masks over there, those—"

"Do you ever take trades?" I cut him off.

"What?" Cooper asked, obviously caught off guard by my question.

A smile danced on Zeta's lips. "What are we talking?"

I knew there wasn't any way Cooper and I could ever afford a rabbit's foot—the price tag was astronomical. It was double what Mom made at the hospital in a year. But if I could trade in a cursed item . . . "A cat," I said. "A scrawny black one."

12

LEAVES OF THREE

"It's too dangerous," Cooper said.

"And the rest of my life isn't?"

Cooper let that sink in for a minute. We were back at the park, swaying on the swings again. The air felt humid, like it was going to rain. The sky was a thick woolen blanket.

"What about your winning streak idea? That could work. It's really awesome that you qualified for the spelling bee."

"Thanks," I said, and shot him a waning smile. "None of this has anything to do with that. I mean it does, 'cause it's all about improving my luck. But things just keep stacking up against me. It's going to take more and more for me to get out of this deep dark hole I'm in. Even if I do win the spelling bee, and get my birthday wish, and pass the Luck Test, what about the broken mirror? What about Wink? I have to find a way to truly be a Lucky. You heard Zeta; if I can trap the black cat and turn her in, she's worth the same as just about anything in the store."

"Yeah, but can you imagine what kind of person would even want to buy a black cat from Zeta? I almost don't want the cat to wind up at Lucky CharmZ. Do you know what I mean? Plus, I just think we should try something safer first—safer for everyone involved. Maybe we could trap a rabbit."

"Right. And why don't we catch a unicorn or maybe a leprechaun while we're at it?" I said sarcastically.

"C'mon, Sadie, I'm serious. I mean, I know rabbits are extremely rare, but so are cats. All I'm saying is that it *is* possible. And maybe we should start by going after something that hops around harmlessly, rather than something that's going to hurl jinxes at us. How are we going to catch a cat without crossing its path?"

Cooper had a point. "Okay. We'll look for a rabbit first," I said, although I wasn't exactly sure what we'd do with a live bunny if we found one. *Are rabbits' feet even lucky if they're still attached?* I pushed the thought out of my head. It didn't matter. The way I saw it, our chances of actually trapping a bunny were pretty much zero to none.

But maybe bunnies and black cats like to frequent the same places, I thought to myself. Just because Cooper was looking for a bunny, that didn't mean I couldn't be keeping an eye out for the cat.

"Let's try Rispin Field."

"Ugh," I croaked. "Why Rispin Field?" Rispin Field was on the far side of the cemetery, just beyond where I'd seen the hand in the bushes. Urban legend said it was named after Charlie Rispin, an orphaned boy who'd died of fever shortly after the cemetery was shut down. A well-meaning aunt had scattered Charlie's ashes behind the cemetery wanting him to spend all of eternity close to where his parents were buried. He'd haunted the field ever since. Unless sent there on a dare, practically no one ever set foot in the field.

"No one ever goes there," Cooper said, echoing my thoughts. "If there's still a rabbit to be found in this town, I'm guessing that it's lying low in Rispin Field."

I considered the idea more carefully. Close to the cemetery might mean close to the cat. Plus, the field wasn't *inside* the cemetery. I wouldn't have to hold my breath. And maybe, just maybe, Wink would see us and wander out. "Okay," I said, hoping it was taking extra long for Mom and Petey to order my cake and that Cooper's parents weren't concerned about where he was, or more important, who he was with.

Cooper dug in his backpack and quickly produced a bag of carrots and what looked like a butterfly net. He raised the small, flimsy green plastic net. "Best I could do," he said. "Maybe we'll catch a baby bunny."

By the time we reached Rispin Field, the sun was peeking through a cloud, and the scenery was almost picturesque with all its wildflowers, knee-high weeds, and a rocky bluff in the background. In the daytime and with your back to the cemetery, it was hard to believe this place was haunted.

"See any rainbows?" I said. "Perhaps we really can catch a leprechaun."

Cooper grinned and calm washed over me. "So how are we going to do this?" I asked. "Should we split up so we can cover more ground, or . . ."

"Let's stick together," Cooper said. "That way if we do scare up a rabbit, we can corner it so it can't get away."

Over the next hour or so, we unearthed several worms and found a few creepy dark holes in the ground that at first looked promising but ultimately yielded no bunnies. We took a break on a log and started munching on the carrots ourselves.

Cooper stared hard at the carrot in his hand, like it held all the answers. "I think my parents are starting to get suspicious," he said quietly.

Now it was my turn to stare at a carrot. I didn't ask if he'd told his parents about the telescope or where he'd been after school the past few days. I didn't think I even wanted to know. Every time the subject of his parents forbidding him to hang out with me came up, I got a sour stomach.

"We have to figure out something soon," he added. "Or else . . ."

"You're telling me," I grumbled.

"Maybe we should try looking for four-leaf clovers instead."

I quickly did the math in my head. The effects of one four-leaf clover probably lasted about a week. Which might just see me through the Luck Test, but what about the remainder of the seven-year curse? I was starting to think my plan really was too short-sighted. There are fifty-two weeks in a year. Fifty-two weeks multiplied by seven years equaled three hundred and sixty-four four-leaf clovers. If there was a patch of more than three hundred and sixty four-leaf clovers in Rispin Field, I was pretty sure we would've stumbled upon it by now.

"Why not?" I said. At least it extended the time I got to spend with Cooper, and from the sound of it, these afternoons together wouldn't be lasting much longer.

Cooper got down on his hands and knees and began slowly making his way across the field, inspecting all the plants as he went. I glanced over my shoulder at the cemetery, as I'd been doing all afternoon, hoping that Wink or the cat would make an appearance. Neither did.

I didn't like the idea of crawling around, the height of the weeds keeping me from being totally aware of my surroundings. Nor did I like the idea of crushing the plant life inside Charlie Rispin's stomping grounds.

Most encounters were rumored to take place at twilight, or just barely after dark. The stories told were of a pale, sickly boy with rosy fevered cheeks, and an old-timer's hat. Some people recalled him as a weeping child. Others said he solemnly beckoned them to follow. Almost everyone agreed that at some point they found themselves standing at the iron bars of the cemetery, not certain how they got there but feeling compelled to fetch the poor boy's eternally resting parents. Perhaps that's what happened to the person who had been reduced to an extending skeletal hand just inside the fence.

I didn't like it, but at last I dropped to all fours and joined Cooper in his search, grateful that we were still hours away from twilight.

We searched for the elusive four-leaf clovers in silence for nearly as long as we'd sought after the close-to-extinction rabbits. We searched until the sunlight began to dim and my knees were sore from pebbles and sticks and who-knows-what-else I'd knelt on in the thick overgrowth.

"Let's go home," I pleaded with Cooper. I'd grown too tired and discouraged to glean any more warmth from his dogged optimism. Plus, I was feeling more and more afraid as the sun dipped a little lower in the sky with each passing moment.

Cooper nodded and rose to his feet. Even he seemed to finally be grasping how futile our efforts were. As he stood, he reached just below his khaki cargo shorts and began feverishly rubbing his knee caps. The skin on his legs was red and blotchy. At first, I thought it was just marked from brushing against shrubs and kneeling on hard, bumpy ground. But when I got a closer look, I could see that it was clearly a rash.

Before my eyes, his skin was exploding with hives, and I could tell Cooper was only pretending that they didn't burn like fire.

"What did you get into?" I asked, concern lilting my voice.

He half grimaced, half smiled. "Leaves of three—let them be! But I'm pretty sure they didn't let *me* be."

I ran close to where he was standing in the middle of a patch of green three-leafed plants. Poison ivy! "Oh, Cooper," I said pityingly.

He was hunched over scratching madly at the blisters, but that didn't stop him from shrugging. "Looks a lot like a clover patch, doesn't it?"

Cooper wrapped his arm around my shoulder as we trudged out of Rispin Field. I'm not sure he really needed my help walking, but having his arm around me did seem to distract him from all the itching. And I was afraid he'd scratch until he drew blood if I didn't keep him moving.

As we walked away, I scanned the cemetery fence one last time—both watching for Wink, and nervous I'd catch a glimpse of Charlie Rispin materializing out of thin air. I didn't see either, but something was watching.

Just inside the cemetery, oval, slightly slanted yellow eyes were reflecting the dimming light. I felt my body tense. I would've tried to lure the cat into the open so I could grab hold of her, but Cooper was already suffering enough because of me. I couldn't risk it. But maybe I could come back later.

Cooper must've noticed that my shoulders had gone rigid. "Sadie?" he asked, and then tried to peer over me to see what had drawn my attention.

"It's nothing," I said as I caught his eyes and flashed him a smile I wasn't feeling. In addition to distracting him from the rash, I wanted to distract him from the cat as well. I blurted out the first thing that came to mind: "So do you have big plans for the dance on Friday?"

I felt Cooper's shoulders stiffen now, too. "No," he answered. But when he did, I noticed that he would no longer look me in the eye.

13

U-N-L-U-C-K-Y

Thursday was the day before my birthday, the day Mrs. Swinton added a fourth horseshoe to the board, and the day of the spelling bee.

Cooper sat with me at lunch. He wore jeans that covered his legs. He said that after a cold shower and some ointment, his rash had almost completely gone away. I didn't believe him. For one thing, he kept rubbing his pant legs together and dragging them up and down along the edge of the bench seat.

When he offered me half of his cupcake, Felicia speared me with a look from the end of our table. Her hair was down and sleek and dark as night, and she appeared as though she was inhaling a whiff of something terrible through her tiny, perfect nose.

When Cooper swiveled his head in her direction, she plastered on a smile and waved jovially. Cooper waved back as he licked yellow-and-black frosting from his upper lip. "The cupcake is from Felicia. Some sort of spelling bee day celebration. She handed them out to all the Luckies before school." As soon as Cooper turned his head back, she started glaring at me again.

My stomach was tied in knots. I was trying not to eat too much in case I vomited onstage. But I made a point of polishing off the bumble-bee-striped treat. And I'm not gonna lie, knowing that Felicia didn't want me eating the other half of Cooper's cupcake made it taste that much sweeter.

When Cooper left to join the Luckies lining up for recess, Betsy slid into the seat where he'd been sitting. "So you ready to wipe that smug look off Felicia's face?" Her brown eyes were alight.

I wished I was feeling half as pumped as she was, but I'd barely had time to squeeze in more studying for the bee after searching Rispin Field. If it hadn't started to rain after I'd walked Cooper home, I wouldn't have studied at all. I would've gone back for the cat.

Felicia and Sabrina stood up from their end of the table and walked over. "Sadie, can you spell *slaughter*?" Sabrina said through gritted, gleaming white teeth.

"Oh, you!" Felicia said, patting her friend on the arm. "I'm far too civilized to slaughter anyone. *Disgrace* on the other hand . . . D-I-S-G-R-A-C-E. There. That has a much more cultured ring to it. Speaking of a disgrace—nice jelly stain, Sadie."

I glanced down at the front of my faded lavender T-shirt. Sure enough, raspberry jelly was leaving a trail as it slid down in one gigantic glob. I'd only taken a single bite out of my sandwich, but, admittedly, my mind had been a million miles away at the time. The deep red preserves must've oozed out without me noticing.

Felicia snickered as I reached for a napkin and attempted to clean myself up, but it only worsened the red smear across my shirt.

"My mistake," Felicia said, turning back to Sabrina, "*slaughter* was the right word. Sadie already looks like she's spilling blood."

I went to the bathroom and turned my shirt inside out, though I wasn't sure that was any less embarrassing. As soon as the Undetermined students returned to the classroom after recess, Principal Lyon's voice crackled over the intercom telling all the spelling bee participants to report to the gym.

Felicia bounded from her chair and proceeded to frolic down the hall. I staggered out of my seat. Nathan Small whispered, "Good luck," and Betsy squeezed my hand as I walked by. My legs felt like I was walking through molasses as I continued to the gym. *M-O-L-A-S-S-E-S*, my brain spelled. It was about all the warm-up I had time for.

Principal Lyon directed all the participants to two rows of six chairs lined up on the gym stage. He steered most of the students to their seats with a gentle hand on the shoulder. When my turn came around, he pointed. "Right there, Sadie, front and center." He was a tall, thin man, with thinning hair, and thin features. I suspected that many of his receding qualities were caused by anxiety.

I took my seat. So much for hiding out in the back. To my right sat Felicia and the two representatives from the sixth-grade Luckies class. To my left sat two fifth-grade participants. The other two fifth graders and all four fourth graders sat in the back row.

After we were situated onstage, the rest of the Luckies filed into the gymnasium, led by their stout, primly dressed teacher, Mr. Barton. He winked at the two Lucky representatives from his homeroom, and then inspected his class. They strolled into the gym in a perfectly straight line and then faced the stage. In unison, every last Lucky crossed their legs and took a seat on the gym floor.

Cooper beamed at me from his place at the tail end of the class. If he noticed that my shirt was turned inside out and that there was a jelly stain seeping through, he didn't let on.

The rest of the gym filled up quickly with every class from first grade on up. Well, not every class. The Unluckies were holed up in their classroom per usual.

My heart droned *flee, flee, flee* in my chest as the air buzzed with excitement and idle chatter filled the space around me.

But I stopped myself from looking for an escape route. I needed this win. *Win the spelling bee. Make my birthday wish. Pass the Luck Test.*

Repeat something enough times, and it will be so. There had to be a superstition that went something like that, didn't there?

Felicia was sneering at me as though she could read my thoughts. *Ha!* she seemed to be saying. *You win the bee? Dream on.*

I inhaled and exhaled through my nose. No. Spelling was concrete. There were correct spellings and incorrect spellings. This wasn't a test of luck. I could do this.

I caught Mrs. Swinton's eye and she gave me an encouraging nod. Betsy did the same. They were a lot alike—both rooting for the underdog.

Principal Lyon shushed the crowd and explained the rules. "We'll be applying single elimination—one misspelled word and you'll be out of the competition. Stand up and speak into the microphone when it's your turn. You may ask for the word to be repeated, for the origin of the word, or to hear it used in a sentence. The words will be given in random order. If everyone is ready, we'll begin."

The principal threw softballs at us for the first round, giving us a chance to get comfortable. My word was *dearth*; Felicia's was *gem*. Everyone survived the first round.

The second round, however, things got a little trickier. I nearly forgot the *h* in *melancholy*, but Felicia had no trouble whatsoever spelling *ballerina*. We both continued onto the next round. Two fourth graders and three fifth graders did not.

I spelled *trauma* correctly on my next turn, but the microphone popped, sparked, and started smoking as I stood at it. We had a five-minute delay while Mr. Barton found and hooked up a new microphone to the sound system.

By the eighth round, it was down to me, Felicia, and both Luckies. Felicia proved to be luckier than both of the Luckies. Her word was short and sweet: *cosmos*—fitting, as the stars always aligned for her.

When it was Jake Miller's turn at the mike, he spelled, "G-E-N-O-R-O-S-I-T-Y." Obviously, *generosity* was not something he was very familiar with. Faith Johnson went out on *cordiality* for similar reasons.

When it was my turn, I barely squeaked by. I had to ask for a definition of *beleaguer* and for it to be used in a sentence. Principal Lyon responded, "*Beleaguer* means to trouble, harass, or beset with difficulties. The Unluckies beleaguer the Luckies."

With narrowed eyes, I spoke into the microphone: "Beleaguer, B-E-L-E-A-G-U-E-R, beleaguer."

Principal Lyon announced that we were down to our final two contestants. As if the entire audience couldn't see for themselves that there were only two people left onstage.

By then, Felicia seemed to be boiling beneath the surface. I'm sure she never expected me to make it this far. Apparently, neither did Fate. As my randomly selected words grew even more difficult, Felicia's only got easier.

I spelled *debauchery*, she spelled *sugar*. I spelled *jeopardizing*, and she spelled *glitz*. Luck of the draw lobbed her words like *lilac* and *diary*. It hard-pitched me: *treacherous* and *mercurial*. But I stayed in. Somehow I stayed in.

In fact, we both stayed in until we'd exhausted Principal Lyon's entire list of spelling bee words. The entire school (minus the Unluckies) stared at us, dumbfounded, as he conferred with Mr. Barton and Mrs. Swinton.

Mrs. Swinton couldn't hide the delighted expression on her face as they broke apart. She discreetly gave me a thumbs-up as Principal Lyon announced that according to the rules, if there wasn't a clear winner at the end of all rounds, then the remaining contestants would both advance to districts. "Fortune Falls Elementary, I give you your co-champions: Felicia Kahn and Sadie Bleeker."

I rose to my feet at Principal Lyon's prompting, and the student body broke into scattered applause. Felicia stood stiffly next to me.

A tie? What did this mean? Could a winning streak begin with a tie? I didn't think so, but it was undeniably better than a loss. Many of the faces I met in the crowd were quizzical, some bordered on disdain. I was, after all, not the type of person they'd pick to represent their school at districts. A few of the Luckies started chanting: *"Felicia. Felicia. Felicia."*

But when I caught Cooper's eye, he smiled broadly and fist-pumped the air.

Felicia noticed and leaned over to whisper in my ear, "Enjoy it now. At the dance tomorrow night, I'll have him all to myself. He did tell you we're going together, didn't he?"

I couldn't stop myself from whipping my head around, but I managed to keep a straight face. I could only hope it was enough to keep her from seeing how much her words stung.

"And next year, when we're both at Flourish and you're at Bane's, you'll be nothing more than a distant memory. *If* you cross his mind at all. Because it makes no difference what kind of speller you are, you always have been and always will be U-N-L-U-C-K-Y."

14

A PERFECT STORM

Despite my failure to annihilate Felicia, Betsy seemed genuinely happy for me. "You did amazing! I can't believe you knew how to spell all those words. I was sure *tsunami* started with an *s*."

"Er, thanks," I said. I'd sort of expected Betsy to ditch me after the spelling bee. Instead, she waited for me after the final bell, and we started walking out of the classroom together.

"Sadie." Mrs. Swinton stopped me. "I know today's tie wasn't exactly the type of success you were looking for, but you should still be very proud. You handled yourself remarkably well under pressure. Regardless of how you do on the test Monday and where you end up next year, that's a very important skill to have."

I found myself mumbling my thanks again and, at the same time, nearly stumbling over my own feet to get out the door. I needed to be outside. I needed fresh air to breathe.

Betsy kept pace with me until we reached the school lawn. "Are you all right, Sadie?"

I nodded my head yes, even though I wasn't so sure. I was still reeling from the not-quite-the-win I needed, and from Felicia's words. Was Cooper really taking *her* to the dance? "I'm just in a hurry," I said. "I have to pick up my brother from preschool."

"Okay, well, see you—" Betsy cut herself off. The silence was uncomfortable. Staying home on Friday the thirteenth was common but not something really talked about.

"Yeah, see you around!" I said, like I hadn't noticed the awkwardness.

Betsy smiled, and we went our separate ways as heavy gray storm clouds gathered in the sky.

When Ms. Summer released the preschoolers, I hung back. I didn't dare cross the particularly tricky stretch of sidewalk with my seven-year curse still activated. I just motioned to Petey's teacher so she knew I was there, and let my little brother traverse the splintered cement all on his own.

"Are you going to wish for Wink to come home, Sadie? Are you?" Petey asked the moment he'd slipped his hand into mine.

"My birthday isn't until tomorrow, Petey. You know that. You also know I can't tell you what I'm wishing for or it won't come true."

All kinds of panic-inducing thoughts started racing through my head. *First I have to blow out all twelve candles. Plus, I have this curse hanging over my head. And just the idea of going to Bane's gives me nightmares. But no matter how hard I try, nothing seems to give.*

I wasn't sure how Petey would feel about me weighing my future over Wink's return if I shared any of my thoughts, so I just said, "I know how much you miss her, though, buddy. I miss her, too."

"We're walking by the fence today, aren't we? I know she'll come if we're both calling her. Or maybe I could—"

"No. No matter what, you are absolutely not going in THERE!" Petey had gone from not speaking to me the night I came back without Wink to incessantly begging me to take him looking for her. He didn't understand why we couldn't just return to the last place I'd seen her, and then search until we found her.

"It's too dangerous," I'd said.

"Why is it too dangerous?"

"Because."

"Because why?"

Five-year-olds do not give up easily. I'd skirted around his questions for as long as I could, but finally I exploded with, "Because she's lost in the CEMETERY. Okay? That's WHY."

Which, of course, just backfired on me. Now as we were

walking home together, he started trying to convince me yet again that I should let him go in. "But, Sadie, Wink might have her foot caught in a vine. But, Sadie, what if something happened to Wink's good eye and she can't see her way home? But, Sadie, I've had four purple days in a row, and I can hold my breath really long. Watch."

He could hold his breath a long time. Scary long. He stopped right where he was in the middle of the sidewalk and held it so long I thought he was going to pass out. He was actually turning purple. At last, not knowing what else to do, I tickled his belly until his curls started to jiggle and he was laughing so hard he couldn't help but suck in sweet fresh air.

"Okay! We'll stop by the fence," I said, glancing nervously at the darkening skies overhead, "but nothing more." It kind of hurt watching how bursting with hope he was as we approached the cemetery. Since Mom had been picking him up from preschool, this was his first opportunity to pass by it since Wink went missing. I could tell he just knew she was going to stick her one-eyed, pirate dog face through the iron posts, wag her tail, and follow us back home.

I made Petey stand a few feet back from the fence. That way, we could call out Wink's name at the same time, and neither of us would have to hold our breath.

"WINK!" Petey cried at the top of his lungs, drowning out my significantly less optimistic yell. But at least I *was* yelling. I missed her so much, and it would certainly make planning how to phrase my birthday wish simpler if she did show up.

My brother might never have given up calling for Wink, if the sky hadn't started to rumble. The storm was getting closer.

"Petey, we have to go," I said. "We can try again—" This time it was me cutting myself off. I'd been about to say tomorrow, but there was no way we were stepping foot anywhere near the cemetery on Friday the thirteenth. "On Saturday," I finished.

My little brother didn't put up as big of a fight as I'd expected. Most likely it was because the thought of being caught in the rain terrified him.

We beat the storm home, and Mom arrived shortly after Petey and I had devoured our apples. She was carrying grocery bags stuffed with black socks, cotton balls, and black feathers. "Help me, Sadie," she said. "We need to get these up tonight."

The wind had picked up, but the ground was still dry. I nodded my head. Cooper and I had plans to meet at the park again. But that was before Felicia told me about the dance and before the sky started grumbling. When I didn't show up, he'd assume it was because of the storm, but it had every bit as much to do with what Felicia had said. I felt betrayed, and that was almost worse than feeling unlucky.

"You stuff. I'll stitch," Mom said.

Petey helped for a little while and then wandered off to play. Mom and I sat at the kitchen table, and I piled cotton ball after cotton ball into the black socks. She sewed them closed with a needle and thread, and then tacked on the feathers. "What do you think," she asked, holding up our first completed specimen.

"Looks like a dead crow to me."

"Good." Mom went back to sewing. Thunder rattled in the distance. I was pretty sure neither of us cared to be standing near a tree when it reached our house. Still, it was important to get the fake crows up early, before Friday the thirteenth actually hit.

Crows are remarkably smart creatures; they don't scare off easily. But, apparently, the sight of their own species hung upside down from the branches usually does the trick. Lucky CharmZ and some of the luck boutiques carry incredible effigies—imitations that look just like dead crows. But, of course, we couldn't afford them, so we had to make our own.

Mom's brow was creased. Her features sagged with worry as she worked.

"I tied for co-champion of the spelling bee today," I announced. Since I hadn't told her about my winning streak plan, I knew the news would make her happy—lift her spirits a little.

"Ouch!" Mom's finger shot to her mouth. She sucked a droplet of blood from where she'd pricked her finger with the needle. "That's fabulous, Sadie! You just surprised me."

After that, I decided to keep my mouth shut. When we'd finished with the crows, we tied long pieces of cord around their necks and carried them outside. I handed Mom the fake birds as she looped the cords over the tree branches and knotted the ends securely. "There. Those should make it through the rain, don't you think?"

"Definitely," I said, though I wasn't sure about anything going the way I wanted it to anymore. We finished just in time, racing inside as the first droplets hit the ground.

As soon as our feet hit the hardwood floor, the phone started ringing. Mom continued the mad dash, sprinting to the kitchen to answer. I ambled in behind her.

"Yes, Mr. Keen, I know you're short-staffed and that a power outage does create a huge problem . . . No. I do value my job. It's just that my nursing exam is tomorrow, and it's also going to be my daughter's birthday. It's not the best timing for me to be up all night working . . . I see. Can you hold, please?"

My mother looked at me, more frazzled and distraught than ever. She pleaded with her eyes. "Sadie girl," she said. Mom hardly ever used my old nickname. I'd always liked it when Dad called me that, but it felt wrong coming from anyone else's lips.

130

"I have to go into work," Mom continued. "It's a night shift. If there was another way . . . I'm sorry, honey. Do you feel comfortable watching Petey?"

I watched my little brother all the time. What she was really asking was if I was comfortable watching Petey alone, all night. In the middle of a raging storm.

Not really.

"Sure, no problem," I said, and nodded my head. I was almost twelve now, old enough to know when uncomfortable things were unavoidable.

Mom kissed me on the head, sinking through my wild curls until her lips connected with skin. "Why does everything always have to hit at once?" she whispered, more to herself than me.

I turned my attention out the window, at the wind and the lightning and the rain, and thought about all the things in my life and all the things, as Mom had said, "hitting at once." Dad used to call that a perfect storm—when all these random, unpredictable things came together to cause one gigantic blowup. Is that what I was headed for?

My thoughts were interrupted when Mom turned back to the phone and said in a low, strung-out voice, "Okay, Mr. Keen, I'll be there in half an hour."

15

CHUTES AND LADDERS

"Chutes and Ladders or Candy Land?" I asked Petey.

"That one," he said, pointing to the board game with jolly children barreling down slides, having a rip-roaring good time. They were obviously Luckies. I sighed, opened the lid to the game, and spread out the board and spinner on the kitchen table between us. I couldn't wait until Petey was old enough to play games that rewarded strategy rather than chance.

My kid brother beat me seven times in a row. I kept landing on the same spot. The spot where the girl falls down, breaks all the dishes, and then goes sliding back to the beginning. Just as Petey landed on the spot where a boy rescues a cat from a tree (a cat!) and shoots up fifty-six places on the board, a clap of thunder boomed so loudly that we both jolted and I knocked my knees on the table, sending the game pieces flying.

As I scrambled to pick up the pieces, my brother ran to the window.

"Petey, back away from there!" I shouted. It wasn't safe to stand near windows during electrical storms.

"But there's lightning!" he said.

"Which is exactly why I want you to move away from the window," I said, trying to rein in the panic in my voice.

"But, Sadie, Wink hates lightning!"

"I know, Petey."

Petey turned back to face me, his fists like small rocks at his sides. "She hates storms, Sadie. I bet she's sad. Sad, like after-Dad-died sad." My brother's face was framed in curls, and with his stark white shirt, he looked like a little cherub. He was so upset, so close to tears, that my heart broke a little just watching him unravel. Behind him, the rain was turning to hail and pelting the window with a vengeance. "We have to find her. We just have to," he pleaded.

"I know, Petey. I want to find her as badly as you do. I swear I do. But we can't go out in the storm. It's too dangerous. Please, come sit down."

Just as Petey began inching back toward the table, I heard the window shatter. The noise was deafening—glass hitting the floor, wind swooping in, blasting the room with all its might. A piece of hail the size of a baseball landed on the hardwood in the middle of the broken glass.

Petey screamed, and I reached out for him. "No!" he shrieked. "Don't touch me. This is your fault. Everything's

133

your fault. You lost her and . . . and . . ." Now Petey was crying, gulping for air, even. "And it's *your* fault Dad died. I'm sick of everything being broken because of you. You're unlucky."

Petey stopped swallowing gulps of air. His face set like stone beneath a stream of tears. I wondered how long he had wanted to say that to me. How long this storm, bigger than the one raging outside, had been building inside his puny chest.

"Petey, I . . ." But what could I say? I couldn't exactly deny it, and the weight of it all was far worse than that of having broken a mirror. Whether or not I lived to see it, at least the seven-year curse had an end to it. Shame was another story.

My little brother turned tail and raced to his room, slamming his bedroom door shut behind him.

I followed him down the hall. I stood outside his door. I stared at the grains in the wood as hail beat down through the broken window in the kitchen, resounding like gunfire. Lightning flashes caused the hallway to flicker from dark, to murky light, to dark again.

One one-thousand, two one-thousand, three one-thousand BOOM. The lightning wasn't right on top of us but close enough. The strikes were probably the worst near the cemetery. *Poor Petey. Poor Wink.* Fate was tormenting me again, and both my brother and my dog were suffering for it.

I lifted my hand to knock on Petey's door but let it fall before I rapped my knuckles. Shaking my head, I sighed and returned to the kitchen. The pieces of hail coming down were smaller than the one that had shattered the window. But they were large enough to leave little divots in the hardwood floor before they bounced up and struck my legs.

My skin stung and reddened from the barrage, but I didn't move. I just waited until the hail subsided and then swept up the mess. I dumped shards of glass mixed with hailstones in the trash. I taped a clear plastic bag across the broken window and then I retreated to my room.

For a long time, I lay on my bed staring at the ceiling wondering if it was going to collapse in on me like everything else. At some point I must've shut my eyes, because the next thing I knew, I was awakening to a world that was far too quiet.

It took me a few fuzzy moments to realize that it wasn't a loud patter of raindrops, or hail, or even a booming crash of thunder that had drawn me back to awareness. It was the quiet solitude of nighttime in the wake of a powerful storm that had roused me.

I remembered going to watch fireworks on the Fourth of July, back before the displays were banned in Fortune Falls because a luckless choreographer nearly lit the entire town on fire. It wasn't the grand finale that was the most deafening but the seconds just after, when the air tingled with emptiness. That's when I felt like I couldn't hear anything—not while the fireworks were exploding.

It was the same sort of tingling emptiness that woke me. I hopped off my bed and ambled over to the window well. I could see through the glass that the pebbles in the bottom of the well were slick and wet and peppered with chunks of hail, but nothing was falling and the sky was a constant, starless black.

It had to be way past Petey's bedtime, and I'd never tucked him in. Never had him change into his jammies or brush his teeth or anything. It was my first time watching my brother all night long, and I was failing miserably.

I trudged up the stairs, wondering if I'd find him with the lights on playing with his blocks or curled up fast asleep on his floor. The answer was neither. He just plain wasn't there. I barreled through the doorway. Pushed pillows from his bed. Searched his closet.

"Petey!" I screamed, racing to the bathroom, then to Mom's room, followed by the living room, and finally the kitchen. My little brother wasn't in any of the places I checked.

Then it hit me. He'd gone to look for Wink. When the storm had died down and while I was sleeping, he'd crept out of the house. I just knew that was what had happened. I knew it like I knew any fact. Like the sky was blue, and the grass was green, and that when thirteen people dined together, the first to stand up would be the first to die.

And if Petey had gone looking for Wink, that meant he was headed straight for the cemetery.

16

GLOOM AND DOOM

I rocketed out the door, calling Petey's name even though I knew he wouldn't answer. I didn't like being outside at night. It wasn't that I was afraid of the dark exactly. (There were far more menacing things to be afraid of when you were unlucky and living in Fortune Falls.) It was that the dark made the wretchedly inauspicious things harder to see. Cracks were harder to see in the dark. Crows were harder to see in the dark. Black cats were harder . . .

Sure enough, at the end of my driveway, the black cat sat waiting like she'd been expecting me. I wouldn't have seen her at all if it weren't for the light I'd left on inside. It was reflected back at me by her insidious yellow eyes.

The thing was, I wasn't even angry this time. I was past angry. I was despondent—so tired of all the gloom and doom that I couldn't even begin to muster any fury.

Petey's voice was echoing in my head. *It's your fault that Wink is lost, Sadie. It's your fault Dad died.*

Now when Petey tripped inside the cemetery—vines reaching out to wrap around his skinny ankles—and when he struggled against them until he could no longer hold his breath, it would once again be my fault. And I couldn't bear the thought of a little, skeletal Petey hand forever reaching for the iron bars.

But even if I had little hope of rescuing Petey, I had to try.

I took a step forward. And then another. I swallowed and then breathed in a little of the dampened earth smell before taking yet another step.

The cat didn't move. She just sat there like she had no other choice. Well, neither did I. I knew my next step would, undoubtedly, cross the cat's path, but I took it anyway.

The cat looked at me, meowed, and then at the very last second, she moved aside. She deliberately sidestepped a few feet, just to get out of my way. It was strange, but there was no time to dwell on it. I wasn't sure how far ahead of me Petey was, but I knew if I didn't reach the cemetery before he went in, it would be too late.

I tore down the sidewalk like never before—never in daylight and certainly not at night. An owl hooted in the distance, and it roiled my stomach. I didn't stick around long enough to hear if it hooted two times more. If it did, I didn't want to know.

Three owl hoots in a row meant death was coming.

My strides were long and swift. With my luck, I'd both land on a crack *and* not make it to the cemetery in time. Then I'd have a missing dog, a dead father, a dead brother, and a mother with a broken back. If that didn't make me the sorriest case of unlucky in all of Fortune Falls, I didn't know what would.

My heart was pounding like a drum as I neared the gates, and my chest felt tight, like it was strapped in a straitjacket. "Petey! Wink!" I screamed at the top of my lungs. "Petey! Where are you?" I reached the gates at last, but no one was there. All along my head had known I'd never make it in time, but my heart must've thought differently for it to shatter the way it did.

Then I saw a torn scrap hanging from a thorn on a long-neglected rosebush. It had shoots growing through the iron fence. Even in the dark, I could see that the cloth was stark white. It had been ripped from Petey's shirt.

My spirits plummeted. I felt small and useless, and I didn't know what to do. I couldn't possibly rescue Petey on my own, but there was no one to turn to for help. Even if I could somehow manage to convince someone to come, there wouldn't be enough time.

By then, I was so desperate, I did a rash thing.

I dashed straight into the cemetery.

At least I had the sense to hold my breath as I hopped

sidelong over the fallen-down gate and landed in the thick overgrowth. Once I was in, there was no turning back.

A crescent yellow moon lingered behind a wispy cloud, spilling a sliver of muted light on all the tombstones. I strained my eyes desperately searching for any sign of movement. Hoping to find a trail of matted-down weeds or broken twigs where Petey's little feet might've plowed through the thicket, I dropped my gaze. When I looked back up, the movement made me dizzy. Not good. I was already beginning to feel light-headed from the lack of oxygen.

I heard the plaza's clock tower bell ringing in the distance. It clanged twelve times and then silence. Midnight. It was officially Friday the thirteenth.

Pressing forward anyway, I blindly wove my way through the headstones and bushes, beside fallen-down crosses, and beneath scratchy tree branches. Except for the rustle of my own footsteps, it was eerily quiet. Insects and creatures of the night had been driven into holes and crevices by the rain. I found myself wanting to scream just to break the silence. To break the panic pulsing through my body and the screeching inside my head, begging for just one sweet breath.

Everything ached.

My lungs burned, and my stomach had squeezed itself into a tight, painful ball. Keeping the air in wouldn't be a possibility for very much longer. I swiveled in the direction the gate should have been, but it wasn't there. No matter which way I spun, I was met with nothing but darkness broken up by gray marble monuments. The monuments all looked the same. Then they began to sway.

Undulating, spinning, giant stones rippled and wobbled in my vision. I'd gone far too long without air. Stumbling and lurching, I reached forward with my hands.

Everywhere I groped my fingers were met with frigid pockets of air. Something icy caressed my cheek as if it could tease me into opening my mouth and letting it in. Walking over the graves had stirred what lay beneath. I could tell they were encircling me, like vultures encircling the dying.

Then I saw the shadowy image of a face—beaklike nose and beady eyes—jeering at me in the darkness. Angry and desolate, I made a swing for it, and my fist connected with iron. Not a face after all. Just an ornate section of the fence, with iron twisted into decorative leaves and vines.

My knuckles throbbed where they'd struck the iron, but I was never so happy to injure myself in all my life. Using the iron vines as footholds, I scrambled over the fence seconds before my diaphragm betrayed me. I wheezed in gulps of cool nighttime air. I fell to my knees and crawled. I made it about a foot away and then collapsed.

For a long moment, my brain shut down. I didn't think. I just felt. The ground was cold and wet beneath me. I shivered.

Then the chill and wetness leached in, and it was me that was cold and wet. I shivered again.

"Petey," I whispered, and tasted salty tears on my lips. Even if I'd had the energy, I wouldn't have wanted to lift my head. Curled in a ball, quakes ran through my body with each new sob.

It started to rain again, but I didn't even care. I just stayed with my knees tucked to my chest as rain splattered down around me and joined the river of my tears.

And then . . .

Then I felt a warm, rough tongue lick my hand.

"Wink!" My heart kick-started with a tiny hum, and I lifted my head. But it wasn't Wink at all.

The black cat released a guttural yowl. She held my eyes with her eerie yellow ones.

The hum I'd felt kindled and built into rage. I sprang to my feet and stomped at the cat. "Come on!" I taunted. "Just do it already. Cross my path. I don't care!"

But the cat just mewed again. This time the sound was full like the moon and sorrowful like death.

"What do *you* have to be sad about?" I sneered.

She withered in the rain. Her scraggly black fur was dripping wet. She trembled the way Wink did at the sound of thunder. "You stupid, wretched thing!" I screamed, and turned my back on her.

I faced the cemetery once more. No, I was the wretched thing—an unlucky, cursed girl standing between a graveyard and a black cat on Friday the thirteenth. My situation was utterly hopeless.

I took a step toward the gate. I didn't bother sucking in my breath. I closed my eyes and inhaled the chill. It numbed my mouth, my throat. Would the frosty fingers of the other-worldly things feel the same as they reached inside me? Would they freeze the hurt, the pain?

It was me Fate wanted, not Petey and Wink, not Dad, not even Cooper. At some point, Fate must have settled on killing me by degrees—ripping my heart out piece by piece as it picked off the ones I cared about most in the world.

I couldn't fathom returning home without my brother. I took another step toward the gate. The only person I really had left now was Mom, and I knew Fate would get around to stealing her from me eventually.

I imagined all the light leaving her sleepy, dreamer eyes when she came back to an empty house in the morning. The worst was that she'd never know what happened to us. Nobody in their right mind would search for Petey and me inside the cemetery. Our bodies would most likely never be found. I thought about how hard Dad's death had been on her, and I stopped moving forward.

If I went back over the gate, Mom would be the one left

alone in the world, and she'd be left forever wondering why. I remembered her sinking her head into my curls, pressing her lips against the top of my head. In my heart, I knew that if she had to choose between having one unlucky child and two dead children, she'd choose me. *She would choose me*, I told myself a second time, *no matter how much pain I cause her*.

I turned around.

The cat was gone, but I didn't care. Through a blur of tears and heartache, I somehow found my way home. I trudged across a lawn sprinkled with black feathers. The fake dead crows had been beaten deader by the storm. Just like me.

17

BLACK CAT

Scratch. Scratch. Scratch.

I thought it was Fate, robed in black, scratching my window with a boney white hand. *Scratch. Scratch. Scratch.*

I opened my eyes. *"Merrooww,"* the cat moaned, staring at me through the glass. She was sitting in my window well, scratching the window with her claw. A strip of white dangled from her mouth.

"Just leave me alone."

If Petey came back, I didn't want to miss the sound of the door creaking open. Not *if—when*. Petey was a Lucky. I was sure of it. He had to have escaped the cemetery somehow. Since I'd returned home, I'd been remembering the many occasions Petey had sidestepped disaster. How often had he moved aside in the nick of time just as I knocked over a heavy lamp, or wrecked my bike, or fell down the stairs in front of him? This was the kid that gum-ball machines poured open for, and for whom soap bubbles landed on skin without popping.

Since I'd returned home, I'd been convincing myself that Petey was still alive.

"Merrowwwww," the cat cried with the white cloth still stuck between her pointy sharp teeth. She sounded like she was dying.

I lurched out of bed and walked over to the window well, intending to pound my fist on the glass until she left. "Go away!"

Then I saw that the cloth in the cat's mouth had been ripped from Petey's shirt. I couldn't tell if it was the same one I'd seen hanging from the rosebush or if it was different. I pushed the question out of my mind. All I wanted to do was touch it—to feel with my own hands something that had rubbed against my little brother's skin not long ago.

I slid the window open, and the black cat scampered in. "Give me that!" I screeched as she evaded my grasp and scurried past me.

I ran after her, through the basement, up the stairs, and to the front door.

When I reached her, she finally dropped the cloth at my feet. When I bent over to pick it up, she mewed plaintively and looked at the door.

I ignored her as I lifted the cloth to my cheek, as I tried to soak in any little, Petey boy smells. A lump formed in my throat.

The cat walked in a circle and mewed again.

I swung the door open. I didn't care about trapping her anymore. I just wanted her gone so I could decide what to do next—stay home and wait for Petey, or go out looking for him again. But instead of darting away as I'd expected, she just stood there waiting.

Only when I chased her out the door did she actually leave, and even then, it was just a few scampering feet, followed by another lamenting meow. Then she stopped again, gazing back at me.

"What?"

"Mew." Two more steps.

I stepped forward and she kept walking. I stopped and she stopped. *She wants me to follow her*, I thought. The cat purred as though she knew I'd finally figured it out. She ran to me, and I kneeled down out of habit, the way I used to kneel down when Wink ran to me. The black cat purred again and nudged the piece of Petey's shirt dangling from my hand with her nose.

It was still pitch-black outside. The sun hadn't even thought about poking its head above the horizon yet. I had plenty of time before Mom came home.

"Okay," I said at last. "What do I possibly have to lose? Show me."

At that, the cat trotted off, and I dashed after her. I wasn't surprised when she headed back toward the cemetery, but then she rounded the corner of the fence and entered into Rispin Field.

I tried not to think about anything other than keeping up with the cat as she wove through the tall weeds. I didn't want to think about whom or what we might encounter in the field or what the cat might be leading me toward. I didn't want to stop out of fear—I *had* to know—but I didn't want to get my hopes too high, either.

The sky was starting to sprinkle again, but for the time being, my tears had run dry.

Every once in a while the cat would glance back, as if checking to make sure I was still following. When I increased my speed, so did she. If the cat had any tail to speak of, I might've been able to lunge and snatch her up by it.

At last, I could tell that she was headed for the rocky bluff at the edge of Rispin Field. *What if it's a trap?* I thought as she trotted straight for a crevice within the natural stone wall. But if what she wanted was to curse me, she'd had plenty of opportunities already.

An overhang of rock above the crevice created an inlet where the rain couldn't reach. I slowed my speed as the cat disappeared around a boulder within the alcove. This was it. One, two, three more steps and . . .

Lying on the ground, behind the boulder, was the pint-size form of my little brother. The cat leapt up on a second boulder and perched herself protectively above Petey as he slept. I ran to his side and stroked my fingers through his curls. "Oh, Petey," I crooned, relief washing over me. "Oh, Petey, you're okay."

The cat mewed approvingly, and something inside me softened. I nearly reached out to pet her, but then I remembered what she was and the peril she was capable of causing.

I drew my hand back just as Petey sat up. He yawned and opened his eyes halfway. When he was sleepy, he reminded me of our mom, and my heart throbbed with the relief of knowing he was safe.

"Why are you here?" he asked. If he was still upset with me, the drowsiness had stolen any evidence of it from his voice.

I charged him with a hug. When I pulled back, I placed my hand on his arm and gently asked, "What are *you* doing here?"

"I followed the boy."

My insides turned to ice. Afraid I knew the answer before even asking, I asked anyway, "What boy, Petey?"

"I don't know. I'd never seen him before. He was wearing a hat. A funny flat hat." He couldn't have heard the woeful story of Charlie Rispin, or else the sight of a boy in a herringbone cap would've sent him into a fit of terror. It would've made his heart race; the way mine did just hearing about his encounter.

"You said not to go into the cemetery, so I didn't," Petey continued, glancing up like this somehow made his disappearance all right.

"But your shirt—what happened to it?"

My brother stretched his shirt out to examine the shredded bottom seam. "I stayed outside the gate to call for Wink. But I wanted to look inside . . ."

"So you went up to the fence."

"Uh-huh. I held my breath. But something grabbed me and I ran." I pictured the thorny rosebush with shoots weaving through the iron posts. It must've snared his shirt as he peered inside. "Don't be mad. Please, Sadie."

I shook my head. "'Course I'm not."

"I ran to the field. That's when I saw the boy with the funny hat. He asked who Wink was, and I asked him if he'd been eating strawberries, 'cause his face looked red like when I eat strawberries."

I could tell Petey's sleepiness was wearing off. He'd let go of the tattered seam of his shirt and was looking up at me with eyes as round as pennies. "He said his parents were inside the cemetery, just like Wink, and we should go in to look for them. But I didn't want to go in. I asked if his parents were dead, and I told him my dad was dead. Then he got a sad look on his face and ran off."

I didn't say anything more as I listened to Petey's story, but I never loosened my grip on his arm, either.

"I wanted to say I was sorry for making him sad, but he wouldn't stop running. I followed him here. But he wasn't here. I don't know where he went. Do you know, Sadie?"

I shook my head. I truthfully didn't know. This night was turning out to be full of surprises.

Petey didn't seem fazed by my lack of answers, nor by the fact that the little boy had disappeared down a dead end path. "Then the rain started again," Petey said. "You know I don't like rain. I was going to go straight home when it stopped. I promise."

I wrapped Petey in another fierce hug. Water was no longer dripping over the edge of the alcove, and I couldn't hear the patter of raindrops splashing down in Rispin Field, either. "It's probably a good time to go," I said, releasing Petey. He nodded in agreement.

We clambered to our feet, but when we stepped away from the boulder, the black cat hopped down after us. Noticing her for the first time, Petey's mouth formed the shape of a little, worried O. "Sadie," he said nervously.

"It's all right," I said. "I don't think she means us any harm."

Charlie Rispin didn't materialize the way I thought he might as we plodded through the damp, muddy field. Maybe his ghost wasn't as dangerous as I'd thought. I supposed it was possible that Charlie had led Petey to shelter, the way the cat had led me to Petey.

Maybe I'd misjudged them both.

The black cat trudged along behind us as we left Rispin Field and as we held our breath to pass the cemetery gate. Every time I glanced over my shoulder, she was lingering just a few feet back. I knew I'd probably regret not trapping her when I'd had the chance, but all I cared about in that moment was getting Petey home before the rain started up again.

18

MAKE A WISH

The black cat slept in my window well. Just for a few hours, because that's all we had before the sun woke us both. I thought about running outside and trapping her before she could escape, but then I noticed how boney her back was, how the outline of her ribs made her sides as rippled as the corrugated aluminum.

"You won't do me any good dead," I said. Then I darted upstairs, found a can of tuna in the cupboards, and darted back down.

As I peeled back the lid, I questioned whether the real reason I was feeding her was so she wouldn't starve to death before I traded her to Zeta or if it was something else. She'd led me to Petey. I felt indebted to her. I shook my head. The thought was ridiculous. Even if it wasn't, I couldn't afford to feel sorry for the cat, to feel anything for her. She was just a means to an end—a way to erase what I'd started when I'd broken the mirror.

I opened my window and set the can inside the well. The cat purred and moved to rub against my hand. I jerked my arm back before she could and slammed the window shut. "Just—" *Just what?* I thought. *Just stay there? Just don't curse me? How about, just don't be nice to me, because I'm only going to trade you in for something lucky.*

Or was I? How could I possibly trade her in at Lucky CharmZ after she'd shown me such kindness the night before? Zeta would sell her to someone who'd use her for bad things. What kind of person would want to own a cat just to hex people? Someone who wouldn't treat her very well, that's who.

If I traded the cat in for something that broke the curse and then went on to Flourish Academy, I'd still have to live with myself. I wasn't sure it was worth being a Lucky if it meant betraying who I was. I'd just about solidified my decision when I heard a knock upstairs.

"Happy birthday!" Cooper cheered when I swung open the front door. Unbelievably, with what little sleep I'd had, I'd almost forgotten that today was Friday the thirteenth *and* my birthday. When that much came back to me, it also came back that I was still angry with Cooper.

I glowered at him. "You're a Lucky. Why aren't you at school?"

Mom was allowing Petey and me to stay home, but any student who didn't feel threatened by the ominous day typically wanted to be there. It was like the pre-party for the dance. The Luckies brought treats to school and basically just hung out with their friends. Some of the teachers showed movies. Mrs. Swinton would be adding a fifth horseshoe to the board.

Cooper faltered for a second but recovered quickly. "You didn't show up at the park yesterday. I was worried. It's your birthday . . . I thought I could be a little late to school. I wanted to check on you . . . Oh, and I have an idea!"

"Okay," I said slowly.

Cooper grinned. "Yeah, so while I was waiting for you at the park I saw this flyer for a carnival that's coming to Fortune Falls next month."

"Okay," I said again, thinking gypsies, fortune-tellers, maybe dancing ponies with lucky horseshoes on their feet . . .

"The games! You can choose a game you've *never* played before and use beginner's luck to win!"

"Uh-huh," I said, my scowl deepening. "And what exactly am I supposed to win? A giant stuffed panda bear?"

"Money!" Cooper said. "You can win money and use it to buy a rabbit's foot or maybe just a horseshoe, but then you can—"

"You're kidding, right?" I scoffed. "That's the stupidest plan I've ever heard. I'm never going to win that much money. And did it ever occur to you that next month is too late. The test is on Monday."

Cooper's face fell.

"You were serious," I said, narrowing my eyes. "Huh, apparently being Lucky doesn't make you smart." I could tell my words stung, but I couldn't reel them back in. I couldn't make myself be nice when Felicia's words still felt like burning coal inside my chest. Not to mention that I hadn't fully recovered from the scare with Petey the night before. I felt raw.

"Wait. I've got a better idea," I added, clipping my words into sharp little points. "Why don't I come with you to the dance tonight? I'll just pretend I'm a Lucky and play a game there. With beginner's luck, surely I'll be all right. What could possibly go wrong? Oh, wait. That's right. You're already going with Felicia."

I knew I wasn't being fair. He didn't exactly deserve to be on the receiving end of all my troubled anger—there were plenty of things besides him fueling it. But I was tired. I was tired of trying to pretend that I could actually turn my train wreck of a life around.

Cooper stared back at me, evidently dumbfounded. "I'm . . . I'm really sorry, Sadie. I didn't think you'd find out."

"You didn't think I'd find out? That's your excuse?"

"Yes. No. I mean, it's not my fault. Felicia's parents called my parents and set the whole thing up. They said that with it being Friday the thirteenth, they were afraid for Felicia to go to the dance alone, because she might encounter someone, um, Unlucky along the way."

"And you agreed."

"No, of course not! I wanted to skip the dance altogether. I wanted to surprise you and show up here to celebrate your birthday. But my parents wouldn't let me." Cooper paused. He seemed to be searching my face for any signs that I was cracking. There weren't, and I wasn't.

He went on. "They say they want what's best for me. I *know* I can make them see that being friends with you *is* what's best for me. But it's gonna take time, Sadie. Please."

"How much time, Cooper?" I was shocked by how hollow my voice sounded. I didn't have the energy for rage anymore. "The test is on Monday. You'll be at Flourish with your Lucky friends next year, and I'll be some girl you used to know. Felicia's right. Just forget it. Forget me," I said, and shut the door in his face.

Terrible, devastating things happened that Friday the thirteenth.

Knives fell from tabletops and slashed unprotected toes. Umbrellas were foolishly carried into houses, and eyes were put out by wickedly sharp points. People behaved in strange, rash ways, as though the day itself had cast a spell upon them.

The most frightening of all, in my opinion, were the birds.

A flock of crows so thick that light from the rising sun couldn't fight its way between them descended on my street moments after Cooper left. When the house grew unnaturally dark, I ran to the window. Even more black feathers were scattered across the lawn this morning, but several of the fake crow wings were flayed open where they hung, still strung from the branches. I breathed a sigh of relief.

A crow on the thatch, soon death lifts the latch.

It killed me that the people with luck dared to celebrate the unluckiest of days with a party. They threw a dance and wore costumes of glittery black-feathered masks paired with dark clothing. For them, there was nothing to fear and everything to gain. The crows always visited Luckies in multiples—twos, fives, or sixes—and brought good fortune right along with them.

> *One crow sorrow*
> *Two crows joy*
> *Three crows a girl*

Four crows a boy
Five crows silver
Six crows gold
Seven crows a secret never to be told

I tried not to think about Felicia with her raven-colored hair, new black dress, and piercing blue eyes—which tonight would be framed by the most glorious feathered mask as she danced with Cooper.

Cooper. I asked him to forget about me, but I wasn't sure if I'd ever be able to forget about him. And I didn't know if that would be a blessing or a curse when I was shipped off to Bane's School for Luckless Adolescents. Would the thought of him sting like pouring salt in an open wound, the way it did now? Or would I be able to picture his smile and somehow feel warmer inside?

I hadn't won the spelling bee and kick-started a winning streak. I hadn't discovered any lucky charms in Rispin Field. I'd decided against trapping the cat. I hadn't been able to do anything to turn my luck around. My last hope was to make my birthday wish, but I had no reason to think it would go my way when everything else had gone so horribly wrong. Not that I wouldn't still try. But it seemed like the best I could do now was make an effort to prevent any more calamities before I was forced to part with everyone I loved.

Mom and I had skipped a few preparations the night before because she had to rush off to work. As she was leaving, she'd laughed nervously and said that we were probably "going overboard" with all the measures anyway. But when it came to precautions, I could no longer think of any as being excessive.

· I hurried to drape black cloths over our mirrors. We owned very few of them, for obvious reasons. There was the mirror in the bathroom and the one above the dresser in Mom's room. They were both securely fastened to the wall, but on Friday the thirteenth, there was an added danger of catching Death itself staring back at you in the reflection. So they had to be covered.

When I finished with the mirrors, I started in on the windows, pulling all the blinds shut to discourage the birds from tapping at the glass.

I paused outside Petey's door. Then I cracked it just a hair. He was still sleeping, and the sound of his breathing hummed in my ears like the sweetest of lullabies—steady, soft, and low. In the pit of my stomach, I felt lingering fragments of the fear I'd experienced when I thought I'd lost him. They jabbed at my insides as if I had swallowed jagged pieces of broken glass.

How could I feel like the luckiest person alive to have him sleeping soundly in his bed and the unluckiest person in the world, all at the same time?

My mom walked in the front door while I was standing outside Petey's room, listening to him breathe. Her eyes were rimmed with dark circles from being up all night working. She was still wearing her uniform, and her curls were a tangled mess. But at least she was smiling . . . and holding a cheap paper horn in one hand and my boxed-up birthday cake in the other.

She blew the horn and said, "Happy birthday, Sadie!" obviously going for cheerful but sounding a little flat.

"Thanks, Mom," I said, knowing that being festive didn't come easy to her. Dad had always been the confetti thrower, the hanger of streamers, and the starter of songs. Mom was content to cut cake slices and make certain everyone had a napkin. Doing it all was a lot to ask.

"Oh, let's just have cake now. What do you say? Why wait until after dinner for dessert when we can have it for breakfast?"

The suggestion caught me totally off guard. I wasn't quite prepared for the candles yet, but I also didn't want to ruin Mom's attempt at spontaneity. Before I could answer, she was bustling into the kitchen and stuffing a dish towel beneath the door to block a potentially flame-extinguishing draft.

Then she added the candles to the cake—putting all twelve in a tight little circle in the center. She did everything she could to ensure my success, all with a smile on her face.

But, behind the smile, there was a deep sadness in her eyes. With everything else, I hadn't really given much thought to how difficult today would be for her.

Not only did she have her exam, this was the first year we'd be celebrating my birthday without my dad.

"It's great. Cake for breakfast sounds perfect."

"Did someone say cake?" Petey said as he drowsily wandered out of his bedroom and came to a stop beside me.

Mom blew the horn again. She really was trying to make this fun. Petey flashed me a grin and then bounded over to the table. He took a seat. I lagged behind. Zeta had said a birthday wish was a good start if I somehow obtained one and if I used it correctly. I'd given it a great deal of thought, but I still wasn't sure exactly how to do just that.

Up until the past week, I'd been absolutely certain that if I managed to make a wish on my twelfth birthday, I'd use it for passing the Luck Test. But now everything was so muddled. Petey was watching me with the most hopeful eyes as I took a seat across from him. I knew exactly what he wanted me to wish for.

But if I wished for Wink to come back, I'd still have the seven-year curse hanging over my head in addition to being unlucky to the core. Yet what were my other options? I wasn't sure I'd even survive long enough to see next school year, so wishing to pass the Luck Test seemed almost pointless now.

Wishing for the curse to end was most likely too lofty a wish. Certainly wishing to be flat-out lucky had to be. Not that that had stopped me when I was at the Wishing Well. But still, I had a better chance this time, minuscule as it was, and I didn't want to be too greedy and have it blow up in my face.

My head hurt from lack of sleep and trying to sort it all out, and Mom was already striking a match to light the candles. All I really wanted was for Mom and Petey to be safe, but once I was out of the picture—at Bane's or . . . otherwise—they most likely would be.

Sitting, waiting for my cake at the kitchen table, everything around me seemed distorted somehow. My vision was foggy. The sound of Petey and Mom singing "Happy Birthday" was muffled by the pounding of my heart, the ringing in my ears. And behind the blinds I'd drawn earlier, the wind began to whip against the plastic covering the broken window.

"Wait!" I wanted to scream. "I'm not ready!"

But my mother was already carrying the cake toward me. I couldn't find my voice before Mom was saying, "Make a wish, Sadie!" She sounded far away even though, really, she was standing directly in front of me as she set down the green pistachio ice-cream cake, ablaze with twelve flickering candles.

Then I glanced at Petey's face, his eyes brimming with

hope again as he waited breathlessly for me to blow the candles out. I thought about Betsy using her wish on *her* brother even though he'd wasted his. Petey hadn't done anything wrong. Even running off into the night—he'd just been following his heart.

I knew what he wanted more than anything in the world, and I felt like I owed it to him. Just because I was Unlucky didn't mean he had to be. I'd cost him a lot in his short life. I couldn't bring back Dad, but maybe it wasn't too late to bring back Wink.

I closed my eyes, sucked in the deepest breath I could manage, praying that my short stint as a jogger had paid off, and thought, *I wish for Wink to come home.*

Just as I was about to let it rip, expelling all the air from my lips in one gigantic puff, a gust of wind tore the plastic sheet off the window, and an icy blast of air whooshed in through the blinds. My own wind withered in one small, pathetic gasp, and I opened my eyes.

Twelve puny wisps of smoke were curling in the air. My stomach sunk like an anchor with the certainty that it had been the gust of air that had blown out all the candles—not me.

19

FRIDAY THE THIRTEENTH

Petey beat me three times at Chutes and Ladders before we switched to Candy Land, and then he beat me three times more. When I drew a sugar plum and slid almost the entire way back to the beginning, Petey began to yawn, and I scolded him, probably a little too harshly. "Cover your mouth!" I chided.

"Sorry," Petey squeaked, scared right out of his yawning.

"The Devil!" Yawning without covering your mouth was like breathing inside the cemetery, only worse. Opening your mouth to yawn gave the Devil a gaping hole to slip into and, unlike the wraiths, his strength didn't wane outside the parameters of the cemetery.

"I know, Sadie. I just forgot."

"You can't forget, Petey. Not today!" I said, still with a sharp edge to my voice. Then under my breath, I whispered, "And soon I won't be around to remind you."

"Sorry," Petey said a second time, and his eyes teemed with tears. My failed birthday wish had been devastating for him. He'd only stopped crying when I'd pulled out the board games, and here I was making him start up again.

First I'd snapped at Cooper and now my little brother. What was I doing? Trying to make sure they wouldn't miss me when I was gone? I gave Petey's curls a soft tousle. "No. It's my fault. I shouldn't have gotten upset."

Petey sniffled. "Can we do something else?"

"Anything."

"Can't we go for a walk, Sadie, please? Just a short one. We'll stay off the sidewalks. I'm sick of being inside."

"Um . . ." I'd been expecting him to say something along the lines of building a castle out of blocks or turning the kitchen table into a fort with blankets and pillows. Mom had grabbed a half hour's worth of sleep and then left to take her nursing exam. She hadn't said not to go anywhere, but she probably would've if she'd known about our trouble the night before.

"Please," Petey begged.

I ran through a quick mental checklist: short walk behind the neighborhood = no sidewalks, no ladders, no umbrellas, no birds tapping at windows or landing on rooftops, no mirrors, no salt to be spilled . . . black cat? *Maybe*. But overall it seemed no more threatening than staying here, attempting to ward off a case of persistent yawning. Plus, how could I not give in to Petey's request? This was probably one of our last opportunities to do something like this together.

What other "lasts" were coming? I'd have to make sure he was prepared to get his own snacks when he came home from school and Mom wasn't here. I'd need to be certain that he knew the safest routes around the neighborhood and that he'd always lock the door behind him. I wondered if Mom would be able to take more time off from work to be with him, but I couldn't imagine that she'd be able to. Perhaps Mrs. Morton from next door could watch him. He was too young to be left alone.

"Okay, but promise you'll stay close to me."

A few minutes later, we exited the front door, watching the sky for flocks of birds as we went. The wind had stopped. Outside was a clear, dull gray—not overcast exactly but not bright blue, either. I nodded to Petey, and we slipped down the porch and around the house.

We took a few steps in the direction that led to Cooper's tree house. Petey bumped right into my back when I made a sudden halt. I didn't want to go by Cooper's, even if he was at school. I turned around and spun Petey by his shoulders, and we both began walking in the opposite direction.

"Sadie, look," Petey whispered as he glanced over his shoulder, "the cat."

Sure enough, the cat was trotting after us.

I gawked at the cursed thing, but she just kept bobbing right along behind us, swinging her nearly tailless backside to and fro as she went. It almost seemed like she was giving Petey a wide berth, as if trying to keep him safe.

"She's kind of like Wink," Petey said. "I mean because they're both missing something. You know, Wink's missing an eye and she's missing a ta—"

"I know what you mean, Petey," I said, cutting my little brother off. "But she's nothing like Wink." Just because I had a soft spot for the cat now didn't mean she wasn't still dangerous. "Ignore her."

I did my best to take my own advice for the next ten minutes, until she snuck up behind me and rubbed against my leg. I nearly tripped over her. "Argh! What are you doing, you dumb cat?" I scolded.

But she stared back at me with big, cavernous eyes and mewed softly. Then with what seemed to be the entirety of her scrawny frame, she rumbled out a sweet low purr that melted the last bit of frost off my heart.

"Well, it's not like my luck can get any worse," I said, and reached down to pet her. The cat arched her spine beneath my hand, rising on her tiptoes as if to soak up every last drop of my touch, and her purr deepened. It was full and steady like a motorboat. Petey giggled, and I couldn't keep my lips from quirking upward. "There. Satisfied?" I asked teasingly, and at the same time thought to myself that it was almost nice having the cat around.

But then she darted in front of us and stopped abruptly in the middle of our route. At first, I thought she was just playing. That she would dash to the side, as she'd done in the past, when we drew near. Yet as we moved forward, the cat held her ground.

"What now, Sadie?" Petey asked. "We can't cross her path."

I was confused. She'd seemed so friendly just a few seconds ago, but now alarms were sounding in my head. "What are you doing?" I asked, half expecting the cat to break into a purr again and demand more petting, but she didn't. She just held our stares with an intense, almost threatening gaze of her own.

"Okay, well, we'll just turn around and go back, then," I said, trying not to let my voice give away how nervous I felt. I didn't want to frighten Petey.

When we turned, the cat darted in front of us again and plopped her backside down in the middle of our path.

"Why does she keep blocking us?"

"I don't know," I said. I didn't understand why she'd help me find my little brother and trot along after us like we were her favorite people in the world, only to then turn around and curse us both the second she had the chance. Even if I couldn't wrap my head around it, that seemed to be exactly what she had in mind.

Well, not if I can help it, I thought resolutely. If she was some sort of henchman sent by Fate to draw me in close before striking, I was prepared to keep dodging.

I searched for a way around the dastardly thing. Wanting to avoid the Fiddlemans' house, the sidewalks, and everything else, we'd gone down a path I wasn't quite familiar with. We were standing on a high point of land that dropped down on one side and was sheltered by an embankment on the other.

If I had to guess, I'd say it was part of the same bluff I'd found Petey in and that we were on the opposite side of the cemetery from Rispin Field. That meant we weren't far from the tracks that ran past the falls and the wood mill on the outskirts of town.

"It doesn't matter. We'll work our way around her," I replied at last. I led Petey away from the dirt path, and we started making our way down the drop-off. It was steep and covered with tall grass and rocks. "Just watch your footing," I said as we turned our steps sideways to keep from slipping.

We somehow reached the bottom without tumbling to get there, and I was more than a little relieved to set foot on flat land. That was until I saw the tunnel just ahead. "Noooo," I groaned. Tunnels were nearly as bad as cemeteries, and it was still Friday the thirteenth after all.

Then I noticed that Petey had suddenly gone completely still.

"It's okay," I reassured him. "It's not *that* big a deal. We can walk around it. We just have to remember to hold our breath as we pass by."

"Shhh!" my little brother said. "I hear something."

I strained my ears to listen, but the only thing I could hear was the swooshing of grass as the black cat leisurely strolled up behind us. I half expected her to pull her little trick again, blocking our escape until we had nowhere else to retreat but into the tunnel. Instead, she just continued sauntering right around us and headed straight in.

Petey's jaw dropped.

"Don't worry, only humans are in danger." I don't know why I said it. It wasn't like I was concerned for the cat, especially after she'd just forced us off the path. "Let's get moving before she comes back," I said.

Petey shook his head. "No. Listen!"

This time, all I heard was the cat mewing, her cries echoing eerily from deep inside the dark tunnel.

"She'll be fine," I said. "Let's just go."

"But it's Wink!" Petey said. "I know it's her. She's whimpering just like when she hides in the bathtub. I swear, Sadie. I can hear her."

"Can't be," I said, and shook my head stubbornly. "You just hear the cat."

"No, Sadie! It's *Wink*. We have to help her." Petey puffed

up his chest and then used every earnest drop in his sweet little soul to plead with his eyes. "Please, Sadie. Trust me. We can't leave her here."

It hadn't been that long since I'd asked him to trust me, and the tunnel actually wasn't that far from the cemetery. What if Wink had come out the back side? Did the cat mean us harm or was she helping out again? "Okay," I said at last. "Okay. I'll go look. Just promise that no matter what, you won't come in after me. If I don't make it out, just find your way back to the path and go home and wait for Mom. Do you understand?"

Petey nodded his head solemnly.

What was with me lately? The cemetery. Rispin Field. Chasing a black cat into a tunnel on Friday the thirteenth. For luck's sake. How did I keep finding myself in these situations when my luck was totally shot? Or was it because my luck was shot that I kept finding myself in these situations? Probably the latter.

I counted to three, sucked in my breath, and dashed into the tunnel before I lost my nerve.

The air was crisp and cool. It smelled like earth and coal and long-forgotten things. The ground was equal parts hard-packed dirt and ramshackle railroad tracks—there probably wasn't a soul in Fortune Falls who wanted to come in here to repair them. With the mill being almost entirely shut down, the trains ran infrequently these days. But the threat of one coming, pulling train cars stacked with logs, hung over me as heavy as the gravity of holding my breath.

My eyes were adjusting to the darkness. I could see deeper within the tunnel, up until a nearby bend. The cat's shrieking had stopped, and I heard nothing but the sound of my own heart pounding in my ears. I decided to press on. My head felt clear, so I thought I'd give it a few more steps. I wanted to be able to say I'd tried my best before turning back. Then I'd have to tell Petey what I already knew—that he'd been mistaken.

As I rounded the corner, I stopped dead in my tracks. I couldn't believe my eyes. Not one, but two forms lay huddled together close to the rails, one decidedly larger than the other. The small, darkly colored one was purring.

I rushed to my dog and ran my fingers down her back. She stared at me with her one good eye and let out an eager, little yap. Other than being a hair slimmer, she seemed no worse for the wear. But if I didn't get out of there soon, I wasn't sure I could say the same about me. I was running out of air.

Tapping my thigh, I tried to convince her to follow. Wink struggled forward but couldn't rise to her feet. It was then that I noticed that the tags on her collar were stuck on one of the railroad ties. It was also then that the tracks began to vibrate and rumble.

My chest was tightening and my head was starting to hurt and now a train was coming. Seriously—a *train*. I nearly came undone. Every last unlucky cell in my body screamed at me to get out. *Now.* But I couldn't leave Wink. I couldn't lose her for good, not after I'd just found her. I couldn't return to Petey empty-handed.

Reaching down, I fumbled to find where the ring on her tags was wedged beneath a nail on the tracks. *Come on, come on, come on,* I chanted silently, feeling more woolly-headed than ever. *Just a little longer,* I told myself, but the ring was lodged tightly. No wonder Wink hadn't been able to escape. No matter how much pressure I applied, it wouldn't budge. I tried the release on Wink's collar, but it was broken, just like everything else in my life. The train whistle blew in the distance.

Being struck down by a train, in a tunnel, on Friday the thirteenth, days after breaking a mirror, seemed a fitting end for someone with my luck.

The ground beneath me shook. It traveled up my legs. My toes, the soles of my feet, my calves, and my hamstrings vibrated along with it. Then my torso quivered and finally, my arms, until I couldn't tell where the rumble of the train stopped and my quakes of fear began.

My life was doomed beyond any shred of hope. Even if I tried to run, I knew my legs would give out beneath me. I just hoped the end would be swift.

I closed my eyes and saw my mother's face and little Petey's sweet smile, and heard Cooper's infectious laughter in my ears, drowning out the thunder of the train.

Then my father's voice came to me in the darkness: "Even if you aren't lucky, you're smart, and that's far more important."

Something hardened inside me then, or maybe patched itself is a better way to describe it. I willed myself to believe him—the way I had when I was younger. I was devastatingly unlucky, but I'd survived. I'd made it this far.

My fingers stopped shaking and the rest of me did, too.

I opened my eyes and took in my surroundings while the cat bounded over to a second set of tracks inside the tunnel. I followed her and pressed my palm against one of the rails. No vibration.

There hadn't been a railroad switch on the way in. Perhaps there was one on the other side. Fuzzy light broke through the darkness near the far end of the tunnel. Without hesitation, I sprinted in that direction, heading straight for the oncoming train.

The sunlight nearly blinded me when I reached the opening. I gulped in fresh air and spotted a switch stand a short distance from the mouth of the tunnel. By then I could see the train engine speeding toward me down the track. I didn't have a single second to waste.

I made a mad dash for the spot where one set of rails diverged into the two tracks that ran through the tunnel. Beside the switch was a long lever and a red-and-green target supported by a stand. The target was made of thin metal plates that split apart like the feathers on the tail end of an arrow—green visible from one direction, red from the other. The target was turned so that the green plates were facing the tracks.

I wasn't sure how to operate the switch, and the train was almost there, not slowing down. I had precious little time to figure it out . . .

Just as I took another deep breath, this time to calm myself, I caught sight of a weathered sign screwed on to the stand. Part of the print had rubbed away so that only meaningless letters were left.

A N TR CK - G   EN PL TE

SI E RA K - ED LA E

My mind rapidly worked to fill in the empty spaces.

MAIN TRACK - GREEN PLATE

SIDE TRACK - RED PLATE

The plates were turned on green, so the train was headed down the main track. I had to toggle the lever on the stand. I had to turn the plates to red before it was too late.

Gripping the bar, I tugged with all my might. Something clicked loudly, and the target rotated to red the very instant a giant whoosh of air swept me off my feet. My eardrums nearly burst as the train whizzed by and then veered off toward the right.

I'd done it!

I'd actually switched the train to the other track.

My body heaved. Shivers and quakes coursed through me, but not from fear this time, from relief. Once I'd picked myself up off the ground and pulled myself back together, I sucked in my breath and raced back into the tunnel.

Wink was trembling and whimpering softly, but she was safe. The train had passed her by.

I didn't try to force the ring out from under the nail again. Without the train breathing down our necks, and with the air in my lungs replenished, I was able to think it through. The tags would never budge, but I could take them apart. I carefully twisted and slid the larger ring around and around a separate one attached to Wink's collar until, miraculously, it came free.

Leaving the tags and the larger ring still wedged beneath the nail, Wink immediately bolted to her feet. Her tail thumped against my leg, and I felt a jolt of energy with her beside me.

I wanted to squeeze her to me and never let go, but first we had to get out of the tunnel. I was feeling light-headed again.

The train was merely a rumble in the distance when we charged into the open. The instant Petey laid eyes on us, his face went from a deathly shade of white to being bright enough to cut through any flock of crows.

It was hard to breathe because I was laughing and whooping with joy, but somehow I managed. I also managed to wrap both Petey and Wink, my one-eyed wonder dog, in a gigantic hug.

I was bursting with happiness.

"I thought you were dead," Petey croaked when we finally broke apart. Then his eyes widened again with worry. "What about the cat?"

I'd forgotten all about her. I glanced back toward the entrance to the tunnel, but she was nowhere in sight. The last time I'd seen her, she'd been perched on one of the side track rails. She had to have moved when the train came. She had to be all right. *Didn't she?*

"She led us to Wink!" Petey persisted.

I nodded my head. "Wait here. I'll go look for her." Just as I was about to suck in my breath once more and charge back into the tunnel, the black cat came promenading out. Not only that, she was carrying something small and furry in her mouth—a rabbit's foot.

20

STARLIGHT

We saw two crows perched on a tree limb on the way home.

Two crows, joy—the rabbit's foot was working already. Still, even joy didn't seem adequate to describe what I was feeling. I felt giddy and bubbly and impossibly light. I squeezed Petey's hand, and we both chortled with laughter. Nothing was funny; it was just beyond understanding that our luck had done such a one-eighty. Wink was back, and the charm changed everything. I didn't want to get too far ahead of myself, but it had to mean the curse was somehow broken.

It meant I could pass the Luck Test. It meant I could go to Flourish and stay with my family. It meant I could still be friends with Cooper. It meant I was having the best birthday imaginable, even if it was Friday the thirteenth!

When the four of us—Petey, me, Wink, and the cat—arrived back at the house, Mom was waiting at the front door with a huge smile on her face.

"I passed!" she squealed, her curls bouncing as she ran to greet us on the lawn. She grabbed my left hand and Petey's right hand and we spun circles together beneath the fake crows. "No more Mr. Keen! No more double shifts! I'm a certified nurse, and I'm transferring to pediatrics!"

Remarkable.

It was all too wonderful to believe. I hadn't merely skirted past Fate's skeletal fingers. Somehow, I'd glided far beyond its reach and brought my family with me.

"Mom!" I said, tugging the rabbit's foot from my pocket. Back at the tunnel, the black cat had set it down on the ground before me, almost ceremoniously, with the loudest purr I'd ever heard humming inside her.

The foot was more than a little grisly—a slender white bone protruded from one end and seemed to have been picked clean. But the fur on the other end was soft and fresh and overflowing with fortune. I didn't want to think about what horrible death the poor rabbit had met. What a sad twist of fate that rabbits' own feet never bring them any luck.

Mom clapped her hand over her mouth in surprise. She was ecstatic to the brink of tears. "How?"

"I'm not sure. I . . ." I glanced around searching for the cat and caught a glimpse of her yellow eyes staring back at me from deep within a bush. *Eerie*, I thought, then, *No. Yellow— the color of sunshine, bright enough to penetrate darkness.*

Since she was safely hidden, an explanation could wait. I shrugged.

My feelings for the cat were too jumbled. I knew it would take time to sort them all out. I'd have to figure out what to do about her soon but, for the time being, tucked away in the bushes seemed like an okay thing. And there was something else I'd been thinking about on the walk home. "Can I go to the dance tonight, Mom?" I blurted out. "Now that I have the rabbit's foot, I'll be safe. I know it's my birthday, but we already had cake. And . . . there's someone I need to apologize to."

Mom gave me a scrutinizing look, but it didn't last long. Soon she was bobbing her head happily. "Why not?" Then she reached up and, in one fell swoop, snatched all the remaining fake crows from a nearby branch and tugged until their strings snapped.

I felt mysterious, and beautiful, and lucky.

The rabbit's foot hung from a black leather pouch around my neck, and I wore black tights and a long black T-shirt, and my coils of hair looked wildly exotic behind my feathered mask. My mom had unstitched all the black feathers from the fake crows and then molded and fastened them together until they formed butterfly wings around my eyes.

As soon as I stepped into the school gym, I gasped. It had gone through an even greater transformation than I had. Small white lights were wrapped around four ladders that stood like Eiffel Towers in the four corners of the gym. The twinkling lights provided the only illumination.

Black gossamer cloth draped the tables and hung from the walls. Boys and girls flitted across the room in elegant masks and dark clothing. It felt like a dream or a nightmare or some blurry place in between.

Someone handed me a glass of bloodred punch. I took a sip. It fizzed and sizzled all the way down my throat as I scanned the room for one masked boy in particular.

When a bone-chilling scream sliced the air, my body went rigid—a response so deeply ingrained, I'd probably never rid myself of it. Around me, everyone else was laughing. It took me a moment to register what was happening. It'd just been a prank. A scare. Someone had spooked a friend with a fake, dangling spider. *Fear for fun*—a new concept for me.

It seemed that danger held a sweet appeal for those whose lives had never truly been marred by it.

Terror forced you to feel alive—made your heart pound and your blood pulse, brought a surge of energy and heightened awareness. Maybe, deep down, the Luckies felt like they were missing out on something. Why else would they throw a party on the most dangerous night of the year, set up ladders in the gym, and dress like omen-bringing birds?

Huh. All these years I'd cowered at home on Friday the thirteenth, wishing I were here. And now that I was here, it all seemed rather silly. A giggle bubbled in my throat at the exact same time a finger tapped playfully on my shoulder.

Cooper.

One of his eyes was covered with a pirate patch made from black feathers; the other sparkled brightly in the Eiffel Tower lights. "You came!" Cooper shouted over the music wafting through the air.

I nodded my head and yelled, "She's back!"

I didn't have to explain who I meant. Cooper's face spread into a grin worthy of the most devious, seafaring rascal that ever lived. "How?"

With the loud music playing in the background, it was impossible to explain everything that had happened, so I simply lifted the pouch around my neck and let him have a peek at the rabbit's foot.

"Does this mean?"

I nodded my head. "The curse is broken."

Cooper picked me up by the waist and spun me through the air, which was not an easy thing to do considering we were nearly the exact same height. I hadn't even needed to say

I was sorry. I could tell by the way his eyes were alight with relief and the way he squeezed me to him that all had been forgiven. "You have to tell me everything!"

Cooper set me back down, laced his fingers through mine, then led me through a door that had been cracked open for fresh air.

Outside, the stars were far more brilliant than the twinkling lights inside the gym. With the door still ajar, the now softer, velvety sound of music provided a soundtrack as I told my story. Cooper's forehead creased with concern as I purged every last detail: my mom being called into work, the window having shattered in the storm, and Petey getting angry at me and disappearing in the night. Cooper held my hand, squeezing harder than he probably meant to as I told him about searching for my brother in the cemetery and later finding him asleep in the alcove. Then about my botched birthday wish and rescuing Wink from the tunnel. He didn't relax until I got to the part about the cat and the lucky rabbit's foot.

When I'd finished, he hugged me to him again. "I can't believe you're here."

I melted against him, resting my head on his shoulder. "I can't, either," I whispered.

Just then, sharp voices rang out from near the entrance of

the school. We slowly broke apart and then quietly crept up behind the bushes to get a peek of what was going on.

A trembling Nathan Small stood on the sidewalk. He wore all black—the only shock of color coming from a four-leaf clover pinned to his shirt. Felicia stood in front of him, blocking the way inside.

"Tell me," Felicia said forcefully, "what do you think you're doing here?"

"I . . . came for the dance," Nathan said.

Felicia shot him a scornful look before dropping her gaze to the clover. Quick as lightning, she ripped it from his shirt. "Where did you get this?" she said, holding it out in front of him. "You're luckless. You couldn't have possibly found it on your own."

Nathan squared his shoulders. "A friend gave it to me," he said and then added, "He has plenty."

Felicia narrowed her eyes and without any hesitation, she dropped the four-leaf clover on the sidewalk. Before Nathan could snatch it back up, she pulverized the clover beneath her shoe. "We don't have room for hapless upstarts in this town," she said. "If the Unlucky think that just because someone shows pity on them, they can attend the same schools, even show up at our dances, they're wrong. It's just going to go badly once the charm wears off."

Felicia paused and then sweetened her voice. "I'm sorry. But you understand, don't you?" She wrapped her arm around Nathan and turned him so that he was facing away from the school. "It's time for you to go home."

Nathan didn't put up a struggle. He merely trudged back down the sidewalk. His acceptance of it all—like he'd been expecting something like this to happen—broke my heart more than anything. Felicia watched him go with a smug smile on her face. When he had disappeared from view, she marched back inside.

I lunged forward, but Cooper held me back. "There's nothing we can do now. The clover can't be repaired, and Nathan is already gone. Don't let Felicia ruin your night, too."

I dropped my gaze to the minced pieces of green on the sidewalk and nodded my head.

"Besides, it's your birthday, and you haven't even danced yet."

I allowed Cooper to lead me back to our original spot just outside the gym. Music still seeped like honey through the crack in the door, filling the starlit sky. I shed my anger with Felicia, as well as the injustice I felt for Nathan, and let the music fill me, too. The night was warm with just enough breeze to cause a gentle rustle in the budding leaves of a nearby tree. The air was sweet with the scent of blossoming flowers.

Cooper took my hand again, and I realized that I hadn't danced since my last ballet recital—since the night before my dad died.

"Okay?" he asked.

I nodded my head. Then I let myself go. The swirling and swaying made me feel giddy again. My skin tingled where Cooper's left hand rested on my shoulder, and mine on his side. It felt almost electric where the fingers of our other hands joined together, forming their own little tower between us.

This is why I came, I thought. Not to dress like a crow. Not just because I had a lucky charm and now I could. I came because Cooper was here.

We danced beneath the starlight until I felt dizzy and light-headed. But, for once, it wasn't the light-headedness of having held my breath too long. If anything, it was from breathing deeply, from finally having the world lifted off my chest.

21

JINX

Even though I'd barely slept a wink the night before, I had trouble falling asleep after the dance. Part of me kept wanting to float up and out of bed with the weightlessness and freedom I'd felt while dancing with Cooper. The other part was being chained down by the seared-in-my-brain image of Felicia crushing Nathan's clover.

No matter how much luck I had, Felicia would always have more. And for whatever reason, she would always use her luck to push down those with less luck. I shuddered to think just how far she and her parents might go.

Would they take charms from everyone they felt undeserving, so that only the uber-lucky had any luck at all? If they could convince others the way they'd convinced Cooper's parents, all the Luckies might turn on those with less luck. What if the town decided Bane's wasn't enough protection? Perhaps the Luckies would find a way to also have the luckless adults, maybe even the very young, separated, too. *Or worse.* Would they do to the Unluckies what had been done to all the cats?

I swallowed a lump in my throat and glanced at the window well. At some point, the black cat had hopped down in it again. The second I slid the window open, the cat began purring and rubbing her boney stub-tailed backside against my hand. Her fur was so soft. As much as I didn't want to make the comparison, I couldn't help but think of all the people who'd never given Wink a chance, never given me a chance, for that matter.

But that was different.

Wink was Wink, I was me, but something about the cat was evil. Or maybe not. I wasn't so sure anymore.

One thing I did know was that she trusted me. It would be easy to trap her now and make a trade. That was *if* I still needed a rabbit's foot—which I didn't. Unless . . .

Perhaps I should still make a trade with Zeta, I thought. If I did, I might be able to do something to thwart Felicia's actions. Otherwise, I knew she wouldn't stop campaigning until all the luckless had been eradicated from Fortune Falls.

The next morning, the cat followed me all the way to Lucky CharmZ, brushing against my legs as I opened the door to the luck emporium. I figured it didn't matter if she was seen with me. People in this part of town were frightened of their own shadows. The last thing they'd want to do is mess with a black cat, no matter how much they wanted it to disappear.

Zeta raised his bushy eyebrows at the sight of the black cat weaving between my legs.

"I want to make a trade," I blurted out the moment his eyes met mine.

"Ha! I see you found Jinx," Zeta replied. "This is the cat you want to trade in? I should've known."

"I—no . . . Jinx?" I said, thoroughly confused.

"That's the cat's name. Jinx. It means something that brings bad luck. She's a lucky black cat, so, you know, I thought it would be cute." I swear Zeta started to blush as he went on with his explanation. "Like calling a big man Tiny, or a timid dog Bear—that sort of thing."

"I know what Jinx means," I said, "but did you say—"

Just then, Chance came barreling out from behind the counter. The cat hissed when she saw the pudgy, little pig. Chance squealed, spun around, and dove back behind the counter for cover. Zeta placed a big hand on his big, bald head. "Ack, the two of them really don't get along."

"I'm sorry," I tried again, "did you say she's lucky?"

"Yep, that cat right there is a Japanese bobtail. A black one like her is rare, and one of the luckiest charms you could ever hope to encounter. I had her imported straight from Japan as a kitten. But she's worthless for selling. Everyone around here has it in their heads that *all* black cats are unlucky. Try telling that to the Japanese Yamato dynasty— longest continually ruling family in the world. And why do you think that is? Black cats. Still, no one will buy her for her luck, and she couldn't hex something to save her life."

Zeta leaned in close to me and whispered, "I'll let you in on a little secret, though, if you promise not to tell anyone."

I nodded my head.

"Even in Fortune Falls, luck often has very little to do with the charm and everything to do with perception."

I glanced down at Jinx. She was intently staring at the spot where Chance had disappeared behind the counter. She was poised to pounce just as soon as the pig poked its little pink snout out again. *A lucky black cat?* I shook my head in disbelief. My judgment of her had certainly been clouded ever since the moment she showed up on my driveway. All thanks to my perception of what I thought she should be, not what she was.

What about all the students who'd perform poorly on the Luck Test? How many of them would wind up luckless simply because they were sorted that way? Betsy seemed to have average luck. Apparently, her brother's luck had been average, too. But at Bane's, they'd both be branded Unlucky, so certainly they'd end up as such.

The levels of grayness in luck never failed to mystify me. I knew I'd never get it all figured out, so I moved on to something I could comprehend. "A bobtail," I said, "so her tail is supposed to be that way?"

The shop owner chuckled. "I bet you thought something took it from her. Another animal? A trap? Nah, that's the tail she was born with. And I highly doubt Jinx would let anything or anyone put their hands or teeth on her unless she wanted them to. Fate knows I couldn't put my hands on her. Shame, because petting her makes you lucky, too—for a spell anyway."

"Oh," I said. It all made sense now. I'd petted her before I'd gone into the tunnel with Wink. Jinx was the reason we'd made it out safely, and of course a lucky cat *would* find a rabbit's foot. "How long does it last?"

"I thought so. She let you pet her, didn't she?" He nodded his head. "Seems like the two of you might just be kindred spirits—both used to being misjudged, perhaps? Well, the extra luck lasts only for a few hours, maybe half a day, but it works every time you pet her. Here, Jinx, come here, girl. Let Zeta stroke your fur for a second?" The shop owner droned on, "Here, kitty, kitty."

Jinx licked her paw, ignoring Zeta until he finally gave up.

"Ah, well, if you want me to take her off your hands, I'm more than willing. But I know better than to demand that you give her back. *Finders keepers, losers weepers* and all that. Even if I can't sell her, she's worth at least two horseshoes. Jinx will come around to me eventually . . . as long as I can keep her and Chance from going at it all the time. That is if you still want to make a trade?"

"Oh," I said. "Thank you. But I wasn't planning on trading the cat. I want to trade this in." I opened the leather pouch Mom had given me for the dance and pulled out the lucky rabbit's foot. "The cat I was hoping to keep," I said quietly.

Zeta's eyes darted back and forth between Jinx and me. He whistled and placed one hand in the other, rippling his tattooed muscles. "She must really like you. Let you soak up quite a bit of luck, I'd say. As far as I'm concerned, she's yours. And you can probably do as well as anyone who aspires to owning a cat. Seems to me, though, they're only interested in owning themselves."

Jinx purred. I glanced down at her and felt my face stretch into a grin.

"Now why don't you tell me what you could possibly want to exchange this supremely lucky rabbit's foot for?"

22

FOUR-LEAF CLOVERS

I'm not proud of it, but my first thought had been to trade the rabbit's foot in for one of Zeta's cursed items. A voodoo doll of Felicia Kahn would've been mighty gratifying. But then I remembered what Dad used to say about only sinking yourself when you travel down a road of anger and revenge. He believed the best way to get even was to get ahead.

I knew I could never get ahead of Felicia in the luck department, but maybe I could level the playing field a little. *For everyone.*

That's why I traded the lucky rabbit's foot for Zeta's entire patch of four-leaf clovers.

When the day of the Spring Luck Test rolled around, I was purposefully tardy. I'd opened my window that Monday morning relieved to find Jinx waiting for her tuna. I spent five minutes stroking her black fur. It was silkier and her ribs weren't so pronounced, now that she'd been eating well.

I waited for the identified Unluckies in the hallway. I passed out a four-leaf clover to every student with downcast eyes and a dejected stagger to their step. Some of them thanked me. Others seemed too shocked for speech. All of them smiled.

I couldn't undo the past. Couldn't change the way they'd been branded. But I could give them a good day, maybe even a good week. And, who knew, maybe some of them would find a way to put an end to their bad-luck streak. Yes, *streak*.

When I walked into Mrs. Swinton's classroom fifteen minutes late, she gave me a forlorn look. A look that said, "I'm sorry for you, Sadie. Sorry that you won't pass the test today." When I glanced at the seven lucky horseshoes on the board and then beamed back at her with a confident, reassuring grin, I think she nearly knocked over her podium.

Sabrina and Felicia tsked as I walked by. I paid them no attention. I was too busy thinking about passing out the remaining clovers in my backpack to all the students who would need them. Once Mrs. Swinton started her morning lesson and Felicia and Sabrina snapped to attention, it was easy.

The fortunate students didn't want anyone to mistake them as being nervous, so their eyes never wandered from the whiteboard.

I'm absolutely certain that Mrs. Swinton caught me sliding a four-leaf clover across my desk to Nathan Small, but her lips barely twitched upward at the corners as she continued on with her lesson.

By the time we'd left the classroom to take the test, four-leaf clovers had been distributed to everyone who might've had the slightest chance of failing. And Felicia and Sabrina had no clue. It wasn't until my peers started winning lottery draws and balls started falling on lucky numbers that they had any idea that the Spring Luck Test wasn't going to go down the way they'd all expected.

Stations were set up around all four walls of the gym. I was directed by Principal Lyon to a table beneath one of the basketball hoops along with a few other students. A roulette spinner sat on my table, and I glanced around to see Betsy being handed a pair of dice at another. A large spinning wheel was being turned at one of the other stations, a ball drop game across from it, and a teacher at yet a different table appeared to be writing down the names of students at her station on paper and then dropping the sheets into a bucket.

I was struck by how uncanny this all felt as the teacher running the roulette table shoved five chips at me. I picked five numbers at random and turned my attention back to the room. To an outsider, it would look like nothing more than a school bazaar, and yet there were so many solemn faces. It was like playing carnival games at a funeral.

The ball was making a *thut-thut-thut* sound as it circled around the spinner and then finally dropped into a red slot marked twenty-five. "That's me," I said, and Principal Lyon's eyes widened with surprise.

"Well, congratulations, Sadie." He wrote my name down and then handed me a red ticket after he initialed it. "Hold on to this," he said. "We'll be collecting them at the end."

The spinner was spun four more times, and four more tickets were handed out—two to kids with unquestionable luck, but the additional two to students with green clovers peeking out of their back pockets.

Then we rotated stations, students spinning around the room as if we were ourselves balls on a roulette table. Every time a pair of dice landed on a lucky roll, or a name was drawn from the lottery bucket, or a ball fell into the proper slot, a ticket was handed out.

Solemn faces broke into smiles, and white knuckles relaxed a bit as piles of tickets grew in *everyone's* hands rather than in just the students who'd been expecting to win.

So, yes, I could've poked a doll in the spine with a needle and watched Felicia cry out and squirm in pain, but that

197

wouldn't have been anywhere near as satisfying as watching her jaw drop when Betsy beat her at bingo.

Most people outgrow temper tantrums around the age of three. Felicia, however, had obviously never been forced to progress past the toddlerhood mentality. Her porcelain skin turned as bright as a turnip, and she actually stomped a dressy patent-leather flat on the gym floor before storming out of the room.

The teachers were too befuddled to notice—distracted by the fact that they were handing out just as many tickets to students with tattered clothing and bandages as they were to those in pressed dresses with amulets dangling from their necks and ears.

When the test was over, the teachers circled around Principal Lyon. Fingers scratched foreheads, fists were raised, and clipboards were shaken. Mrs. Swinton tittered almost gleefully. Finally, the huddle broke apart, and Principal Lyon made an announcement. "In an unprecedented occurrence, the wins have all been evenly distributed. Not a single student has failed the Spring Luck Test. Therefore, we've decided to add an additional class of Luckies. We will have not one but two classes of Luckies for the remainder of the school year. Both classes will move on to Flourish Academy in the fall."

I was shocked by the roar of applause that followed the principal's announcement. Simon Swift fist-bumped Nathan

Small, and I was reminded that not all of the more favorably fated students shared Felicia's opinion of the luckless.

She'd calmed herself enough to return to the gym by then. But her eye was twitching, and I was pretty sure she'd replay the whole temper tantrum for her parents later that day when she broke the news. I could only imagine how many calls Flourish Academy was going to receive from the Kahn family before I ever arrived.

For now, I didn't care, because my superb luck hadn't worn off yet. Cooper, Betsy, and I were all assigned to Mrs. Swinton's class for Luckies along with Daniella and some of the former Undetermineds who were all now in possession of a four-leaf clover. Felicia and Sabrina, on the other hand, were moved to Mr. Barton's class.

One month later, the Kahns still hadn't been able to force a retest, and since I'd officially passed the Spring Luck Test, I was allowed to participate in the district spelling bee.

Jinx waited for me in my window well the morning of the bee. I fed her, like I always did, but when she moved to rub against my hand, I didn't let her, even though the last of my four-leaf clovers had shriveled up and died weeks before. "Uh-uh, Jinx," I said. "Sorry. Not today. I have something I have to prove."

The cap came off the carton and I dribbled orange juice on my blouse at breakfast, and the new bike Mom had bought me as a belated birthday present after she'd gotten a raise had a flat tire. I had to walk to the Fortune Falls Plaza for the spelling bee, but that was okay. I just watched my footsteps and made sure not to land on any cracks.

A stage was set up in the middle of the grassy square, and Felicia's parents were in the audience, staring me down as I took my place in a seat next to their daughter. The rest of the participants were students I didn't recognize—champions of their own elementary schools and future classmates at Flourish Academy—but all of them smacked of good fortune.

In fact, I wasn't sure if Felicia was more unsettled by my presence as co-champion or by the glimpse of the competition she'd face next year for queen of the Luckies. Either way, she was definitely scowling when Cooper and Betsy took their seats in the audience and held up fingers that were crossed for me instead of her.

The district bee lasted for over three hours. For the final hour, it was down to just Felicia and me, but the rules stated that at this bee, there could only be one champion. Ultimately, that was me. All the luck in the world couldn't help Felicia spell *chiaroscurism* correctly.

When the officiator handed me the trophy, the welded-on handles broke off in my hand and the heavy bronze cup slid and landed on Felicia's foot. Her parents came unglued and rushed the stage.

"Sorry!" I said, but I don't think they heard me through all of Felicia's wailing. They were grumbling loudly about needing X-rays as they carried her off the stage. I didn't think they'd be any happier when they arrived at the hospital and Felicia was treated by a woman whose name tag read *Caroline Bleeker, RN*.

I'd just won the district spelling bee and that felt better than passing the Luck Test even. This I'd done all on my own, without any charms or luck, and that felt like an even greater triumph over Fate.

I knew that without any strokes of luck garnered from Jinx, I was undoubtedly still Unlucky. But that was okay, and it didn't seem to matter at all to Cooper and Betsy. They charged me with congratulatory hugs as soon as the Kahns had cleared the stage. At the same time, I caught a glimpse of something small and black streaking past the Wishing Well.

Zeta had been right. I couldn't really lay claim to Jinx, but maybe what we had was something more. Something like what I had with Cooper, and Betsy, and Wink.

The following year would be interesting, maybe even unbearable at times when I brought my horrendous luck to a school meant only for Luckies. But I knew I'd be all right. I had friends. And friends truly are the luckiest charms of all.

Acknowledgments

Like many authors, I struggle with perspective when it comes to my own writing. It's a little like getting ready for a date without a mirror. I can choose my favorite outfit, pin up my hair, and smile brightly. However, if I can't see my reflection, I can't tell whether or not I have loose strands, a piece of spinach stuck in my teeth, or if my undergarments (ack!) are showing. That's when a trusted friend is needed to gently point out the eyesores.

Mallory Kass, my friend and editor extraordinaire, you not only lent your discerning eye to this story—you poured the entire foundation for *Fortune Falls*. Without you, this book simply would not exist. I am the luckiest of all Luckies to be able to work with such a generous, endearing, enthusiastic, and dazzlingly smart ally.

I'm deeply indebted to the rest of the Scholastic crew as well. It is a tremendous privilege to work with people who bring so many magical books to young readers. And I'd like to give special recognition to the jacket designer, Ellen Duda, and illustrator, Melissa Manwill, for creating such a striking cover.

My agent, Ginger Knowlton, you are such a patient and gracious advocate. For that you have my never-ending thanks and admiration.

I had an embarrassing number of false starts with this novel, and credit my insightful critique partners, Tara Dairman and Lauren Sabel, with finally getting me set on the right track. I'm so glad we've banded together, along with all the other fine Colorado authors in our growing bunch. It is a vibrant community, and I glean a great deal of creative energy from it.

Matt, Ethan, Logan, and Lucas, you are my four-leaf clover, my inspiration, my everything. My love and gratitude for you knows no bounds.

I also have a fortuitously long list of family and friends, ever offering encouragement and support. For the sake of time and space, I am unable to include everyone here, but please know that all of your names are written on my heart.

Above all else, thank you, God, for the many blessings, and for designing people with an insatiable thirst for stories.

About the Author

Jenny Goebel is the author of *Grave Images* and The 39 Clues: Doublecross Book 3: *Mission Hurricane*. She lives in Colorado where, if she balances precariously on the edge of her bathtub, she has a lovely view of the Rocky Mountains. She shares this view, and her home, with her husband and three sons. Visit her online at jennygoebel.com and on Twitter at @jennygoebel.